MOON
OVER
MANHATTAN

Also by Larry King

Love Stories of World War II

Anything Goes! What I've Learned from Pundits, Politicians, and Presidents (with Pat Piper)

How to Talk to Anyone, Anytime, Anywhere: The Secrets of Good Communication (with Bill Gilbert)

When You're from Brooklyn, Everything Else Is Tokyo

Powerful Prayers

Future Talk

Daddy Day, Daughter Day (with Chaia King)

Champions

The Best of Larry King Live

On the Line

Tell Me More

Mr. King You're Having a Heart Attack

Tell It to the King

Also by Thomas H. Cook

Fiction

The Chatham School Affair

Instruments of Night

Places in the Dark

The Interrogation

Breakheart Hill

Mortal Memory

Evidence of Blood

The City When It Rains

Night Secrets

Streets of Fire

Flesh and Blood

Sacrificial Ground

The Orchids

Tabernacle

Elena

Blood Innocents

Nonfiction

Early Graves

Blood Echoes

Editor

Best American Crime Writing (with Otto Penzler)

MOON OVER MANHATTAN

A Novel of Mystery and Mayhem

LARRY KING
&
THOMAS H. COOK

A PLUME BOOK

PLUME
Published by the Penguin Group
Penguin Goup (USA) Inc., 375 Hudson Street,
New York, New York 10014, U.S.A.
Penguin Books Ltd, 80 Strand, London WC2R 0RL, England
Penguin Books Australia Ltd, 250 Camberwell Road,
Camberwell, Victoria 3124, Australia
Penguin Books Canada Ltd, 10 Alcorn Avenue,
Penguin Books India (P) Ltd, 11 Community Centre, Panchsheel Park, New
Delhi—110 017, India
Toronto, Ontario, Canada M4V 3B2
Penguin Books (NZ), cnr Airborne and Rosedale Roads,
Albany, Auckland 1310, New Zealand
Penguin Books (South Africa) (Pty) Ltd, 24 Sturdee Avenue,
Rosebank, Johannesburg 2196, South Africa

Penguin Books Ltd, Registered Offices: 80 Strand, London WC2R 0RL, England

Published by Plume, a member of Penguin Group (USA) Inc. This is an
authorized reprint of a hardcover edition published by New Millennium Press.
For information address New Millennium Press, 301 North Canon Drive,
Suite 214, Beverly Hills, California 90210.

First Plume Printing, June 2004
10 9 8 7 6 5 4 3 2

Ⓟ REGISTERED TRADEMARK—MARCA REGISTRADA

CIP data is available.

ISBN 1-893224-57-0 (hc.)
ISBN 0-452-28522-4 (pbk.)

Printed in the United States of America

PUBLISHER'S NOTE
This is a work of fiction. Names, characters, places, and incidents are either the
product of the author's imagination or are used fictitiously, and any resemblance
to actual persons, living or dead, business establishments, events, or locales is
entirely coincidental.

To the people of New York City, in triumph and tragedy, examples for us all.

—Larry King and Thomas H. Cook

FOREWORD

As many of you know I am a born and raised New Yorker (Brooklyn). Over the years, my career has taken me all over the country, and I've been living on the West Coast for some time now, but my heart has always remained in New York.

My friend Tom Cook, on the other hand, is a born-and-bred Southerner who now lives in Manhattan and has grown to love his adopted city. Tom is a wonderful writer, an Edgar Award–nominated author, who doesn't flinch from the darker side of life in his work. Who better to collaborate with? I had wanted to write a mystery for some time. I was turning over a plot about missing children in my mind, a topic very near and dear to my heart. I knew Tom would be the perfect person to work with. For several months we kicked around plots and ideas, toying with storylines.

Then the whole world changed in the blink of an eye on a perfect fall morning. In the dark days after 9/11 we commiserated with each other, along with the rest of the country, over the terrible damage inflicted on our city. Soon we cheered the remarkable, resilient spirit of its indomitable residents and took heart. New

York would endure. It was bowed but not broken. My heart swelled with pride as never before for my beloved hometown.

A new seed was planted. There had been more than enough darkness and terror. Tom and I now were inspired to create a lighthearted tribute to all the crazy, wonderful characters who inhabit New York and make it the greatest city on earth. We wanted to write a caper, something light and funny, a celebration of New York and New Yorkers.

A small-time hustler who dreams of crossing the bridge and being a big shot in Manhattan. A sleek, beautiful mistress on Park Avenue. A hard-bitten private eye who bemoans the newly Disneyfied, family-friendly Times Square. A rich, spoiled private-school teenage girl and her dopey boyfriend from the projects. Even (ahem) a rich, famous talk show host. We mixed all these characters and many more up in Manhattan and let them loose.

Moon Over Manhattan is the result. I had a great time working with Tom on it, and he deserves the lion's share of the credit for his terrific writing style. It is our hope that the love, admiration and affection we both feel for New York and its people shine through. Enjoy.

Larry King
March 2003

MOON
OVER
MANHATTAN

PART I

HOBBES WHO?

THE TRUTH ABOUT WITTGENSTEIN

Allison Vandameer

Goonie could kiss like nobody on earth, Allison decided as she drew her lips away and let her head loll back to rest on his shoulder. Goonie could kiss so well that he'd driven all the other great kissers—even Harrison Dillard whose tongue whipped around like a lizard's tail—from Allison's mind. The fact is, she'd rather kiss Goonie than any boy on earth. Well, except for Eminem.

"So, Allison," Goonie breathed tentatively, his eyes still glazed by that long last interlude, but with a clearly more elusive game in mind, "Whadya think?" He paused. "Think," he repeated.

"Think," muttered a second time was a syntactical tic Allison had dubbed the "Goonie Echo," and which she loved because each time Goonie did it, it made her father, the esteemed Arthur Vandameer, host of *Speaking Truth to Power*, and one of the nation's best known, and most tragically underappreciated television commentators, THAT father, wince.

Allison lifted her head. "Oh, Goonie, I can't," she purred.

Goonie looked hurt, as usual, looked positively wounded in fact, like a guy who'd gotten his leg shot off . . . or worse.

Allison released a world-weary sigh. Well, wasn't that the way it always was? She had that kind of effect on guys. One look at her and they died of hunger. They swooned and died of yearning. Just like Catherine Earnshaw in *Wuthering Heights*, a book she'd secretly read because she'd not wanted to give her father the satisfaction of letting him know that she was actually reading a classic, and so a book whose cover she'd carefully switched so that the esteemed Arthur Vandameer had glanced up from the dinner table to observe his only daughter, the sole heir to his intellectual legacy, deeply enthralled in a picture biography of the artist formerly known as Prince.

Yes, she, Allison, was just like Catherine Earnshaw in *Wuthering Heights*, the aforementioned Allison repeated to herself, only this time it was the guy who was dying of frustration, which, in Allison's view, was a lot better.

Anyway, one kiss and they were hers. All manner of men. The doorman was hers. Arthur's friend Bernard was hers. Any male dinner guest was hers. With a drop of the eyelid and a pucker of her bottom lip, she could make any male do her bidding. She shrugged in resignation to her power. It was a way of life she would have to endure forever, a painful, life-altering force she couldn't avoid or in any way cast aside. She was a vixen, a femme fatale, the type of girl people wrote about in songs and poems. Romantically speaking, she was the horn of plenty, though she'd never given more than a little nip of the apple. And never would, she concluded, until she met the one guy her father really hated.

Which went a long way toward explaining Goonie. Sure, he was a great kisser, but that wasn't what kept Allison running her fingers through his at times rather distressingly tangled hair. The great thing about Goonie was that he drove her father nuts.

Her father, Arthur Vandameer, seen every night in eight million homes, interviewing, it seemed to Allison, everyone but God. Worse than that, "Art," as Allison called him when he wasn't in earshot, was a history nut who knew all about battles and dates. Which, at the moment, made Goonie even more the perfect choice, since, outside the tiny space of his personal history, Goonie appeared entirely unaware that anything had ever happened anywhere at any time, an ignorance so deep Allison had no doubt that if asked to name an important historical event, the aforementioned Goonie would recount the time he'd thrown-up a corndog on Coney Island.

Best of all, Goonie not only had a ready-to-hand ability to drive Art crazy, he had an almost unlimited potential for doing so in the future. He didn't plan to go to college. The only book he read (an authorized biography of Tony Orlando, digest version) had lots of pictures, and since it weighed in at nearly a hundred pages, Allison had little fear that Goonie would finish it in his lifetime, or even that of the nearest solar system. And to put the cherry on top, he was utterly clueless when it came to current politic developments, even the most recent ones. He didn't know the name of the vice president, for example, and the only reason the president's name came readily to mind was because he sometimes used it to describe a certain female body part.

"But we're in love, right?" Goonie pleaded. "And when people are in love they . . ."

That was the Goonie Full Stop, and it occurred each time Goonie lost his train of thought. Which was often, even though the train was never that long to begin with.

"They . . . you know," Goonie said.

Allison knew all right, but no way was she giving in to what Goonie wanted, which was sex. But then that was all boys ever wanted, Allison had long ago concluded, at which time she had instantly hatched her strategy in the battle between the sexes: *Never give a man what he wants!*

"So, whadya think?" Goonie asked. "About it."

That was the Goonie Mid-Pause, an annoying habit of breaking a sentence into two small parts with a pause in between. That one really drove Art nuts. He practically whirled around in his chair while he waited for Goonie to attach the two emptily rattling cars of his, well, thought-train.

"I mean," Goonie clarified. "You know."

Allison squinted. "I can't Goonie," she repeated, this time with the firmness requisite to terminate any further discussion.

Thus restricted, Goonie began to sulk.

Allison stroked his face. "You need to write that note, Goonie."

"Whuh?"

"That note we talked about."

"Yeah, but . . ."

Allison bounded from the sofa, marched into her father's impressively book-lined office, retrieved one of his assorted Mont Blancs and returned to the spacious living room where Goonie sat, mysteriously toying with his pants.

"Did you bring the paper you were supposed to?" she asked as she handed him the pen.

Goonie nodded ponderously, the hard labor that lay ahead of him now resting fully on his shoulders. "How many words?" he asked as he drew the crumpled paper from the back pocket of his vastly oversized jeans.

Allison looked at him scoldingly. "It's just a note, Goonie," she reminded him. "Not a manifesto."

Goonie appeared to think a "manifesto" was something mechanical, a car part, for example.

"Short," Allison said, trying to contain her exasperation. "Make it short."

"Yeah, okay," Goonie said. He flattened the paper out on the antique table that rested before him. "Short," he repeated, as if trying to find a way to put the word in the note.

"Start with 'dear,'" Allison said.

Goonie stared at her blankly.

Allison frowned. "Dear," she repeated. "The one like 'precious,' not the one in the headlights."

Goonie looked as if this had cleared up a momentary confusion. He placed pen to paper, then stopped and looked up, the enormity of the task weighing on him even more heavily. "Do I—(Goonie Mid-Pause)—have to, Ali?"

Mercy fluttered briefly, like a moth in Allison's head, then was promptly burned to a crisp by a far more urgent need. "It'll drive Art crazy," she said.

Goonie nodded. "Okay." He glanced at the paper, a thin, nearly transparent stationery bordered in bright orange. There was an equally garish drawing at the top, an elephant scratching its head with its trunk as it spoke into a large word-balloon, "If you ain't an elephant, write it down here." For a moment, Goonie's feeble sense of the inappropriate kicked in. "Shouldn't I write this on nicer paper?"

"No, you shouldn't, Goonie," Allison said sternly. "Now write."

With a shrug, Goonie gave in to the inevitable, and in a halting, jerky script, penned his elopement plan for Arthur Vandameer's only daughter.

Arthur Vandameer

Arthur Vandameer was rich, famous . . . and miserable. The wealth came from his family fortune, the fame from his nightly televised political commentary, and the misery from his daughter. Through the years he'd grown adept at downplaying his good fortune. He described himself as "homeless" because he lived in a suite of rooms in the Pierre Hotel. His fame was meaningless, he argued, because it was fleeting. He did not make news, he only commented upon it. He would never be president of the United States, or even a lowly

senator from New York. His task, and he continually ridiculed it to anyone who would listen, was to "second guess" what the "first guessers," the ones who really did things, did. This was, he claimed, a wholly fruitless endeavor, a dreary sideline quarterbacking that could only be of service in a world where time went in the other direction, and so you had a chance to correct the error before you made it. The fact that time, in fact, did not go backwards, made him irrelevant, he said, a reverse Nostradamus, the dreadful opposite of a prophet. "I don't know the point of me," he told Madelyn Boyd, the only woman who still agreed to have him around, "Or if I even have a point."

The fact that, physically speaking, Arthur's "point" had not proven to be in satisfactory good working order on this particular evening had done nothing to enliven Madelyn Boyd's generally depleted store of human sympathy, and because of that she was in no mood to hear any more from Arthur Vandameer.

"Arthur," she said, rising from the bed. "Maybe you'd better go. I have a. . . ."

"Headache?" Arthur inquired. "Surely not that, Maddie."

Madelyn wrapped the red silk kimono around her ample but by no means unattractive frame. "How's Allison?" she asked.

Arthur groaned.

"What's the problem now?" Madelyn asked, now seated at the vanity, her brow slightly furrowed as she wrestled with the admittedly thorny problem of multiple combs.

Arthur ticked off his grievances. "Poor grades. Bad attitude. A boyfriend who's. . . ." Arthur stopped himself immediately, careful that nothing he said about Allison's latest offering might possibly reflect upon the fact that Goonie was . . . well . . . of Hispanic-American heritage. "Who comes from an unfortunate background," Arthur said. "I mean, educationally speaking."

"But what about Allison?" Madelyn asked absently, the comb now moving smoothly through her hair. "She's not on drugs, is she?"

"No."

"Never gotten pregnant."

"No."

Clearly Madelyn believed that considering what might befall a teenaged girl, Arthur, with typical undeserved good fortune, was getting off very easily indeed. "So what's the problem?"

Arthur started to enumerate that very list of problems, then noticed a small blemish on his chest, brown and slightly raised, and thus, incontestably, a harbinger of death.

"I think you're quite lucky with Allison," Madelyn added, now reaching for a different comb for the finishing touch.

Arthur fingered the brown spot, trying to recall if he'd ever seen it there before.

"A gem, if you ask me," Madelyn said.

Arthur looked up, his eyes oddly stricken as he pressed down on the alarming blemish, his mind grimly coming to judgment on the life he'd led so far. "Nasty, brutish and short," he ruminated darkly.

Madelyn looked at him in the mirror. "What's the boyfriend's name?"

Arthur shrugged. "His full name? Joselito Castillo de la Mancha Diaz. But quite appropriately, Allison calls him Goonie."

Madelyn laughed. "Well, just remember, they thought Einstein was goofy."

"The difference here," Arthur said, now running through the names of various physicians, trying to decide if he should first see a dermatologist, or go directly to the oncologist he was certain he'd be sent to anyway, "The difference here is that Einstein wasn't."

Madelyn ran the comb through her hair and marveled at just how lovely she was. Forty-three, and gorgeous. A little dot where her nose had once been. And on her face, despite all the work, no more than a look of perpetually mild surprise. "I think you should give the girl a break," she said.

"And you've had how many children?" Arthur asked. "The number 'zero' comes to mind."

Madelyn brought her combing ritual to an abrupt halt. "Let's not get snotty, shall we?" She glanced at the diamond-studded watch she'd placed on the vanity a few minutes before, a gift from the recently deceased Lawrence Phipps, who, despite that little issue with the pantyhose and black garter-belt, (his, not hers), had been a super lover. And at least, unlike Bridges Blake, he'd never shown up with a suitably elegant Crouch & Fitzgerald briefcase brimming with sexual aids, most of which, as Madelyn now unpleasantly recalled, had required both batteries and some assembly.

"Don't you have to be home, Arthur?" she asked. "For that reporter?"

Arthur shrugged. "A style page writer is hardly a reporter," he said.

Or at least not until recently, he thought sourly, because almost anyone could call himself a reporter these days. Jennifer Cattrell swam into his mind, though he hadn't wanted her to. It was an affront, really, the way he'd been taken in by those perfect teeth and large blue eyes, the fall of her long blond hair, that fawning attitude he'd have easily been able to dismiss had he actually been a great man, rather than what he immediately decided he was, an empty vessel, a bag of hot air, a rich kid who'd accomplished nothing on his own, and so on, forever, in an infinite descent into self-loathing.

"Arthur, cheer up," Madelyn snapped. "You look positively . . . depressed." She jerked open the top drawer of her vanity, retrieved a small plastic bottle and tossed it to Arthur. "Elavil," she said. "You might ask your doctor for a prescription."

Arthur placed the bottle on the bed. "I avoid mind-altering drugs," he said.

Madelyn laughed crisply, then ticked off the incontestably mind-altering drugs Arthur made no effort to avoid. "Vodka. Gin. Brandy. Scotch. B&B, and especially Port. Especially vintage. Especially Dow's Vintage Port." She whirled around on the vanity stool. "Anyway, you'd better get dressed for that reporter," she said a little impatiently, though careful not to mention the fact that Carlton Powers was due to appear in less than an hour. She clapped her hands. "Come now, get dressed," she said in the same voice she used to discipline Pookie, her mean-faced little Pekinese.

"All right, all right," Arthur said. He wearily pulled himself from the bed, and in horror realized that, although otherwise completely naked, he was still wearing one sock. Jeez, he wondered, what could his mind have told him at that moment of undressing. *Okay, stop it, Art, you're naked enough, for Christ's sake.* Suddenly the blemish on his chest no longer seemed important. It was senile dementia he worried about now. For a moment he lingered on his approaching madness, years of finding his contact lenses in the freezer, serving steak-in-a-glass to distinguished dinner guests, thinking Allison was his grandmother.

The last didn't strike Arthur as all that bad. If he could only think of Allison as anything but his daughter, much of his life's steady ache would instantly vanish.

On that thought, Arthur silently dressed while Madelyn returned to her preening.

They kissed at the door a few minutes later, then Arthur walked out of Madelyn's sumptuous brownstone and into the glittering New York night. Up the street, he could see the great stone façade of the Metropolitan Museum. A Munch exhibit had just been installed, and standing now in the darkness, facing the great silent building, Arthur Vandameer thought of his daughter, cupped his face in his hands, opened his mouth, and released, in melodramatic imitation, his own silent scream.

IPSO FACTO

Roy Bumble

From the window of his Queens apartment, Roy Bumble watched the towers of Manhattan rise jaggedly along the western horizon. By distance, they were quite near, a few miles, no more, but to Roy, Manhattan remained as remote as London or Paris or any of the other great cities he glimpsed with zero interest as he surfed past the Travel Channel in search of old reruns of the *Match Game*.

Roy's wife Bea licked the foamy pink residue of her dinner Slim-Fast from the side of her mouth and peered into the empty can. "Strawberry's not bad," she said.

Roy Bumble closed his eyes and dreamed of having caviar at Petrossian. He'd order the Beluga, he told himself, and let the bums have the Seruga. He'd wear a nice Armani suit, pay the tab with Amex Platinum and walk back to his place in the Dakota with a sleek woman fashion designer. That was the life he wanted, and it could only be lived in Manhattan. Living in Manhattan, he thought, would be like running with the bulls at Pamplona. Only it would feel like that every day. He would be a player, a guy who mattered, part of the in-crowd. He would be . . . A GUY WHO LIVED IN MANHATTAN!

"My goodness," Bea Bumble blurted.

Roy's eyes shot open.

"My goodness," Bea Bumble repeated as she slapped at a pink stain across the front of her housedress, "I just washed this thing."

Roy returned his gaze to the distant towers. He'd always dreamed of making a killing that would secure him a little window in Gotham's fabled skyline. Was that so much to ask? Roy asked.

Evidently, because, try as he might, he'd made absolutely no headway in securing even the merest portion of Manhattan real estate.

The problem, to repeat, was money.

And the problem with money, to repeat repeatedly, was that it was hard to get very much of it.

Early on, Roy had realized that the easiest means of obtaining sufficient money to purchase a Manhattan apartment was not open to him, since his only inheritance would be the vegetable peeler his mother had inherited from her mother, which made it a genuine antique, according to Roy's mother, but which, after watching several episodes of *Antiques Road Show*, Roy had sadly determined to be only a shanty-Irish artifact whose value was pretty much summed up by the preceding adjective "sentimental."

For this reason, whatever money Roy gained in life, he would have to gain it himself.

Which was another problem, since Roy had always

known that when it came to the pursuit of wealth, his direction would have to be at a slant. This fact was undeniable. Roy would never be a titan of industry, since he didn't have all that much industry, himself. There was also the problem of having no discernible talent, or even much in the way of skills. The years had also taught him that luck was in short supply when it came to Roy Bumble, a fact each new lottery drawing painfully confirmed.

As to the slant, Roy had tried several. He'd invested in a few of his brother-in-law's inventions ($3,500), bet on a horse named Speed Trap ($1,000), and even put money in a Russian silver mine ($2,500). In all three cases, the return on Roy's investment had been disappointing. As a matter of fact, when he calculated the results, he inevitably came up with a loss of precisely $7,000.

Roy shook his head and took a long draw on what was left of his cigar. *New York*, he sung flatly under his breath, *if you can make it there. . . .*

But how could he possibly make it there, he wondered. One thing was clear. A job would never get him anywhere. What Roy needed was a score.

This was not a new thought. In fact, as Roy admitted, he'd been looking for a score for forty-five of his forty-eight years on earth. As a teenager he'd thought of boosting cars, but rejected the idea for lack of mechanical ability. He'd rejected cutting the heads off parking meters for pretty much the same reason. He'd considered counterfeiting, but for a man who could barely draw a stick-man, the art of engraving was clearly daunting. Other scores required weapons, but on the one occasion Roy had actually handled a gun, he'd been unable to master the intricacies of the safety lock. And so the sad, sad fact, Roy decided as he continued to stare wistfully at the unattainable towers, was that he was a conman without a con, and what could be drearier than that? If you were honest and poor, well, at least you were honest. But to be a crook, and still be poor, that was just plain pathetic.

Still, if he ever wanted to live in Manhattan he had to do something, and this mysterious something had to be a scam. But not just an ordinary scam. A scam run on a Somebody, a Big Somebody—that is, A GUY WHO LIVED IN MANHATTAN.

Bea Bumble suddenly started. "You're gonna be late for work, Roy," she said.

Roy glanced at his watch, then back into the apartment where his Sherry-Netherland uniform hung like a lifeless pelt beside the front door, dark blue with gold epaulettes, the one grand and sparkling thing inside the room.

Harry Stumbo

Harry Stumbo hated almost everything. But the thing he hated most was change. Particularly change in the neighborhood.

He glared at the whirling lights of Times Square. *You'd have to be Mickey Mouse*, he thought sourly, *You'd have to be Mickey Mouse to like this frigging place*.

That was the truth of it. Times Square was no

longer Harry's part of town. With sweet nostalgia, he recalled the streets of the old Times Square. By old, Harry meant no more than a decade before, when he'd slunk around Times Square like a rat in a sewer, usually looking for some runaway from Nebraska, a girl pushing sixteen, with long blonde hair, bright blue eyes, and a mind so open her brain all but fell out onto the gritty sidewalk. Wheat, the pimps and muggers who swirled around Port Authority at 42nd and Eighth had called them—wheat ready for the pulling.

For Harry, those were the days when the Deuce had been worth the ticket. You came out of some lousy theater like a guy out of a foxhole, everybody staring at you like they were measuring you for a coffin. You lived as a mark, you lived like an animal in the jungle, everybody looking to take a bite out of you. And so you kept your eyes peeled to any movement in the brush, and your furry little paw on the licensed piece in your jacket pocket, and you were alive, by God, you felt every breath because it might be your last. He grunted. Jeez, what a numbnuts joint the Deuce was now. Blue-hairs with theater programs, pregnant mothers pushing strollers, guys with cameras loosely slung over their shoulders rather than wound around their neck like hangman nooses, and worst of all, a damn huge McDonald's right in the middle of the street!

The Deuce, damn it, was safe, and that steamed Harry like nothing else on earth. The Deuce was safe as a Vermont cow farm, safe as Sister Evangeline's third grade class, safer than Anchorage, Alaska, the paper said . . . and Harry Stumbo frigging hated it. "Jeez," he moaned under his breath as two twin girls in frilly pink dresses, both giggling madly and with pigtails flying, swept past Harry and sailed up the street toward the glittering marquee of *The Lion King*.

Harry stopped and stood glaring at the marquee. Then the urge overtook him and he fiercely grabbed his crotch. *Lion King this!* he thought under his breath as he stormed ahead.

Thought, mind you, since Harry rarely actually spoke. In fact, Harry Stumbo was, by most accounts, the

world's most silent man, his spare interrogatives and responses generally reduced to one word, and offered only at those unfortunate times when body language proved insufficient to get the point across.

And so now, silently, Harry whirled northward on Eighth Avenue and elbowed his way through the glitzy crowd until he finally plunged through the door of Smith's Bar on 44th.

"Usual," he said to the bartender, then glanced about with a fleeting sense of satisfaction. At least Smith's hadn't changed. Which was just great as far as Harry was concerned, since any change in New York these days served to make the places worse by making it better, and therefore more detestable to Harry.

Alone among the dives around Times Square, Smith's had maintained its legendary dinginess, the smell of corned beef and cabbage so strong it sometimes overwhelmed that first sniff of Harry's usual, a Dewar's, straight, no chaser, a drink favored by a clear majority of Smith's regulars.

The regulars, Harry thought, what a group. Cops and firemen and here and there a couple of old theater types, but only the theater types who knocked back Dewar's, not these new theater types, with their frozen Margaritas. No, that bunch was laughing it up at Blue Fin, the swankiest of the trendy joints that now crowded around Times Square, laughing it up and sipping Campari while they tried to decide if maybe they should have sushi at Kodama, or just share a Power Bar so as to keep their pecs all tight and shiny.

Jeez, Harry moaned inwardly. It was one thing for the Deuce to change, but did it have to change LIKE THAT?!

The bartender brought him the drink, a big smile on his face.

"Smile?" Harry inquired.

"You ain't heard," Felix the Bartender announced triumphantly.

Harry shrugged.

Felix the Bartender's smile widened with pride. "We're fixing up the place," he crowed.

Charlie Moon

Every outfit needs a sane one, and in Manhattan, the sane one was himself. So thought Charlie Moon.

Charlie only had to look out the window of his small office at the *New York Daily Register* to know just how sane he was. Below, the sheep scurried around like chickens with their heads cut off. Well, that was a mixed simile, but Charlie knew what he meant. They went to jobs they hated, then home to families they hated, then took breaks from all this misery by going on vacations to places they hated with people they hated. Charlie shook his head at the sheer folly that swirled around him, and on those rare occasions when his thoughts turned dark, wondered why the poor, hopelessly pissed-off bastards didn't blow their heads off just to get it over with.

Charlie stood up from his desk, walked to the window, and stared down just to reassure himself that things had gotten no better since he'd arrived at this stark conclusion. Nope, he decided, his eyes peering down from the fortieth floor, Charlie Moon was right again. The ants were scurrying about, mindless as spawning trout, obeying the very laws of human entrapment that Charlie, by his superior wisdom, had skillfully avoided.

Of course, Charlie also knew that not everybody had the same high opinion of his conclusions about life.

For example, there were those who argued for enduring love, a concept Charlie dismissed as pure hogwash. Love endured like fruit endured, first it softened, then it went to rot. If you married for love, which, according to Charlie, was usually based on sexual desire, then love would inevitably dwindle as desire faded. If, on the other hand, you married for comfort or convenience, then the fade had already occurred, and so you simply started the marriage at the end and stayed there.

Either way, Charlie opined, it was a dead horse. And so in matters of love, Charlie thought, moving heedlessly towards a split infinitive, the solution was to continually prime the pump, which he did as often as he could find someone to, so to speak, grab the handle. By this means, every night was a honeymoon, except that with break of day the no-longer-blushing bride was on her way out the door, taking all prospect of future alimony—not to mention children, mortgages and heady educational expenses—with her. And what, Charlie wondered, could be better than that?

Charlie's thoughts on death were similarly sane, according to Charlie. If you died believing that there was something beyond death, then that was good because, if there wasn't, you wouldn't know it anyway. And if you died believing that only oblivion followed death, then that was good too, because if there were something beyond death, you'd be pleasantly surprised, and if there wasn't, well, hell, you'd be in the same boat as the others, blissfully unaware that you would be a stone cold nothing for all eternity.

So there it was, love and death, the two things people considered life's greatest mysteries, and he, Charlie, had long ago solved them both. He smiled and let his eyes lift toward the moon that now hung silently above Manhattan. Great mysteries, my ass, he thought.

Best of all Charlie was sane on politics, a proof he'd proved time and again in books and articles before finally taking his latest gig at the *Register*. He'd written on war and peace, the great social issues of his time, and in everything he'd ever written, his wisdom had shown through.

He was still considering his own miraculous sanity when Toots Malone popped into his office. "Boy Wonder wants to see you, Charlie."

Tobias Kenmore Phelps, aka Toby the Boy Wonder, was the son of Seymour Watson Phelps, esteemed paterfamilias of the Phelps clan as well as the CEO and majority stockholder of the media conglomerate that owned the *Register*, along with six radio stations, two horse farms and one acutely dysfunctional brassiere factory. Toby (affectionately referred to as See Less by

the perennially disgruntled employees of the *Register*)
was a twenty-six-year-old Harvard-trained silver spoon
whose mental processes, according to Charlie, were
about as orderly as a mound of linguini.

"Me?" Charlie asked, jerking a thumb toward his own
person.

"You," Toots said, then sailed on down the corridor,
leaving Charlie behind his desk and, he suspected,
some form of eight ball Boy Wonder had just put in
front of him.

Okay, he'd been summoned by Boy Wonder, and
Charlie Moon was far too sane not to recognize that he
had no choice but to show up when sent for by the
aforementioned youthful miracle. In the phrase
"dumb-ass boss," according to Charlie, the only relevant word was "boss."

But none of that did anything to ameliorate the feeling of dread that had been growing in Charlie since the
instant he'd been summoned to Boy Wonder's office.
The problem, he knew, was that he wasn't a promising
young reporter anymore. As a matter of fact, he wasn't
a young anything anymore. On most papers that
wouldn't have been a problem, but Boy Wonder had
made it clear in a thousand different ways that he
wanted a new readership for the *Register*, a young, hip
readership. As a result, the Theater Section now
reviewed mostly off-Broadway theaters, particularly
the ones in Alphabet City, where hordes of NYU stu-
dents and hip young professionals hung out in tiny,
dimly lighted theaters watching irate young women
chew the cardboard scenery along with the Collective

Male Ass. The Music Section hardly paid any attention to Carnegie Hall, while the latest concert of Screaming Anybody was reviewed with the kind of mock intellectual bombast that had formerly been reserved for Ph.D. theses on Rod McKuen's verse. And as for the movies, the *Register*'s new young critics concentrated on action flicks and date movies, leaving the rest of the film world to languish in a lame sidebar known as "Also Opened This Week."

Worst of all, Boy Wonder clearly believed that celebrity news was the only kind that sold papers. Why have Colin Powell discuss world politics, according to the aforementioned miracle child, when Snoop Doggy Dogg was available to discuss the current state of booty?

So what it came down to, Charlie decided, was that he needed a celebrity youth angle. A celebrity-pube-scoop, as he'd come to call it, though he had no idea what it might be, or even whether he'd recognize such a story if it hit him in the face. He knew only that he was sinking at the *Register*, going down like a deflating balloon (or perhaps like the following overwritten, extended and none too sensible description), and that he needed a burst of hot air to lift him up before his career got snagged on the dark mountain range he saw looming straight ahead of him in the impossible distance of an equally extended horizon.

"You wanted to see me, Tobias?" Charlie said after politely tapping at Boy Wonder's door.

"I do, I do," Boy Wonder sang. "Please, Charles, have a seat, won't you?"

All of this was said without Boy Wonder once lifting top teeth from bottom.

"So, Charles," the boss added. "Have you been well?"

"Yup," Charlie said, then wondered if he should have said, "Yup, sir."

"Good, good," Boy Wonder said. He knitted his hands together and leaned back in a leather chair that made him look like Jack in the Giant's hand.

"You do know Jennifer Cattrell, don't you, Charles?"

Charlie nodded. Jenny Cattrell was the girl—oh-excuse-me-the-woman—or-should-I-say-female-human-person—who ran the style page and thus, according to Charlie, used up most of her inconsiderable brain power trying to decide if Santa Fe was really out, or just out in Chelsea.

"Well, unfortunately, Jennifer is indisposed," Boy Wonder said.

Charlie immediately imagined Jenny on the toilet, looking puzzled.

"Under the weather," Boy Wonder added.

Now Jenny was sitting in bed with two strands of Kleenex dangling from her nostrils, but still puzzled.

"Which brings me to you, Charles," Boy Wonder went on. He unknit his fingers, but knit his brow. "Because I'm in something of a bind."

Charlie wished he had a toothpick to chew, because this was getting to be a long haul.

"You've heard of Arthur Vandameer, of course," Boy Wonder said.

Charlie offered a crisp nod. "The commentator, sure,"

he said, "Left-wing liberal. Thinks the prisons should provide bodybuilding equipment to homicidal maniacs." He stopped, now aware that he'd probably gone too far, since most of the blood seemed to have abruptly drained from Boy Wonder's usually baby-pink face. "The tree-hugger," he added because it seemed a milder description of the very Arthur Vandameer whose bleeding-heart world-view Charlie had once ridiculed as "Johnny Appleseed on acid."

"Tree-hugger?" Boy Wonder wondered.

"Didn't he dub that woman who perched in a pine for six months Thomasina Jefferson?" Charlie inquired.

"Yes, he did," Boy Wonder said. "You disagree?"

Charlie dared not answer, since, he supposed, Boy Wonder had probably snuggled up to a few spruces, himself.

"I know you've had disagreements with Vandameer in the past," Boy Wonder said. "But I trust you at least respect him?"

"Sure," Charlie answered. Which was a lie, since Charlie had not the slightest respect for Arthur Vandameer because he was, in Charlie's view, a whiney, hand-wringing spokesman for every left-wing social hallucination, a man who clearly believed that there should be no such thing BUT a free lunch, that all criminals had "issues," and who, worst of all, denied that the secret to maintaining the social order was, as Charlie well knew, keeping a tight grip on the short hairs. If anybody was going to get free bodybuilding equipment, according to Charlie, it should be the cops, although it would be easier, as he'd once written, simply to equip them with medium-range ballistic missiles.

Charlie had most powerfully espoused his SHORT-HAIR THEORY OF SOCIAL CONTROL in his famous article, "Arming Ophelia." In that still-discussed piece, Charlie had argued that girls should get small-arms training for the last four years of high school, then be given nine millimeter automatics along with their diplomas. Boys should just get the sheepskin, along with a sobering exhibition of female firepower. That, he wrote, would pretty much end the problem of rape and sexual assault, since, according to Charlie, the average guy couldn't get it up with a gun-barrel in his mouth. Should this program be initiated, he had also argued, the wife-battering statistics would certainly take a dive, and the male practice of shooting birds at "women drivers" would disappear from the face of the earth. As to the inevitable loss of offending males, Charlie had simply asked, "Who'll miss 'em?"

Boy Wonder loudly cleared his throat. "I'll grant that Thomasina Jefferson was an unfortunate choice of words." He waited for Charlie to respond. When he didn't, he cleared his throat again, this time even more loudly. "But on to the other issue. The situation is thus. Jennifer was due to interview Mr. Vandameer at nine o'clock this evening. She's doing a piece on night views of Central Park, and evidently Vandameer has an impressive one."

"Night Views of Central Park," Charlie repeated, the way someone might say "Dog Crap Floating in Gutter."

One of Boy Wonder's eyebrows arched like the back of a fluffy blond inchworm. "Someone has to do the piece," he said. "Given the situation being thus."

Charlie's stomach drew into a defensive knot, and not only against Wonder Boy's curious syntax. "I don't do style." He cocked his head playfully to the right. "I don't even have any," he added with a self-mocking smile that he hoped might prove disarming.

Boy Wonder's eyes looked like missile silos. "Pierre Hotel," he said. "Nine o'clock."

Charlie ran the numbers instantly. This was a defining moment, he knew. You were either a reporter or you were a fluff-jockey. The issue was integrity. This conclusion inexorably led him to a second set of categories. You either had a job, or you didn't. The issue was money.

Sanity carried the day.

"No problem," Charlie said.

PASCAL'S WAGER

Allison Vandameer

Allison recalled the note again as she sat beneath the gilded equestrian statue of General Sherman, the classic façade of the Plaza Hotel rising majestically just to her right. She knew who General Sherman was, but the real power of knowing such things was in pretending that she didn't when Art gingerly made his little inquires into her bank of knowledge. So several weeks before, when the two of them had been out walking and Arthur had pointed out the statue of General Sherman, Allison had

rolled her eyes, claimed she had no idea who the general was, then hazarded the guess that since he was riding a horse, he was mostly likely "from some old-time time, like maybe, nineteen-twenty?"

Allison now delightfully recalled the stricken look that had appeared on her father's face at that moment. It reminded her of the even more amusing occasion when she'd identified a photograph of Winston Churchill as the road manager for *NSYNC. When Arthur had shaken his head in hopeless consternation, she'd pulled a defensive sulk and blurted out that she couldn't be blamed for making such a mistake since the guy in the photograph "was all fat and puffy," like the aforementioned road manager and Jeez, why should she know who "Winston Church-Hill" was, anyway, since he really didn't MATTER anymore. "I mean, God, the guy's been dead for like . . . two hundred years."

She felt a wave of stinging annoyance wash over her. Arthur! He really sucked at being a father. And the only way she could get back at him was to give the impression that she was a complete idiot. And so, when Arthur talked about history and books, quoted Lord Acton to the effect that those who didn't know history were doomed to repeat it, she inevitably fell into her dumb-blond act by peremptorily dismissing "Lord Action" as just another dead guy. And besides, she went on, he was wrong! Allison Vandameer wasn't going to repeat anything! Well, except maybe tenth grade. But her being held back in school wasn't so bad, she said. Some of the best people were held back. Speaking of which, she'd added in a horrifying aside, she was thinking of getting a tattoo.

Now Allison took a deep breath, peered up at the lighted windows that rimmed the uppermost floors of the Pierre, and thought of the note she'd so cleverly left just where Arthur would see it when he stepped into her room. Perfect, she thought, the perfect way to stick it to him. Even more clever was the placement, which happened to be neatly tucked between a McDonald's cashier application and a Butthole Surfer CD.

The plan was to make Arthur miss her, make him appreciate her, make him be good to her, and most important, make him let her go to film school at UCLA instead of Harvard, or Columbia, or some other place where she'd be forced to study something she didn't like, and after four years graduate with a degree in something she didn't like, then have to get a job doing something she didn't like, and in the end, as she supposed Lord Acton must have known, live a life she didn't like.

And what was the point of life, if you never enjoyed it, Allison asked herself. She thought of Arthur, the sheer lack of enjoyment in his life, that sour face he always wore, as if someone had just farted at the dinner table and who, he'd suddenly realized, was none other than himself. He'd always looked put upon, but it had really gotten worse since the last of his three divorces. But then it was probably the sheer lack of enjoyment that had sent Arthur's third wife to Katmandu where she still lived, chanting or something. Allison thought about Gwendolyn Grahame, her latest stepmother, the one who, at thirty-nine, was still looking for herself.

According to Arthur, Gwendolyn was a "lost person," and Allison suspected that this was true, even though the little cards she received from Katmandu were nice enough. The odd thing was that Arthur hadn't seen it coming. She recalled the day two years before when she'd come home from school to find the apartment empty, save for Arthur. He'd been standing in the living room waiting for her, looking all abandoned and confused. He'd said only that Gwendolyn had left him, but that she would be in touch as soon as she "got to wherever she is headed." Through the whole thing, Allison remembered, Arthur had had this baffled look on his face. Jeez, she thought now, here he was with Gwendolyn gone, and he hadn't seen the slightest sign that she might do this really drastic thing, pack up and split for Katmandu, an act that Arthur could only think of as a complete rejection of himself, and which only Goonie considered "cool."

Goonie.

Where was he, anyway?

Allison glanced at her watch. He should have been here by now, the plan being to hole up with Goonie for a few days, then return, still unmarried, but only because she had started thinking about film school at UCLA, which meant—though she wouldn't have to say it outright—that for Arthur the choice was either to send her to UCLA or back to Goonie.

Goonie.

She looked at her watch again, then at the gilded equestrian statue of General Sherman, the exact spot

where she'd instructed Goonie to meet her at precisely
six p.m.

Where was he anyway?

Goonie

Goonie glanced at the statue of General Sheridan,
looking like a guy in a cowboy and Indian movie, just
like Allison said. Sure, he'd forgotten the general's
name, but luckily his father worked at Discorama on
West 4th and had told him that there was this statue of
a general, whose name, he thought, began with "Sh."

From this, Goonie had reasoned that the General
Sheridan statue had to be the statue Allison had designated as their point of rendezvous because what would
be the point of having TWO statues of generals in
New York City?

With this reasoning safely unchallenged, Goonie sat back on the bench and relaxed, perfectly content that he'd gotten it right and that Ali was probably on her way to him. Either that, or her father was blocking her.

For a moment he imagined Arthur Vandameer, whom he'd never heard of before Ali had pointed out what a big-name celebrity he was, standing at the door, facing Ali down, demanding that she go to her room, which she wouldn't do without a fight, but might not win, because, after all, a father was a father, and Goonie knew that if his own father ever blocked his way, his way would just be blocked, that's all, because Javiar Jose Esperanza Gomez took no crap from any kid, much less his own.

But Goonie had gathered that Arthur Vandameer was no Javiar Jose Esperanza Gomez. As a matter of fact, to the extent he had any impression of Allison's father, it was that he was a wimp. The facts, Goonie thought, justified this conclusion.

First of all, Arthur Vandameer's latest wife had left him, which if Javiar's wife had tried to leave him, all hell would have broken loose, and there would be no Mrs. Javiar Gomez sitting lotus-position in some temple in Kalamazoo or wherever it was that Mrs. Vandameer was currently sitting, exotic, or anyway, according to Ali, with lots of chanting and finding yourself.

Second, if Goonie's sister had ever once opened her mouth to Javiar, the way Ali opened hers to Mr. Vandameer, the aforementioned sister would end up eating soft food for a month.

Goonie glanced at his watch, realized that he'd forgotten to put it on, which was no problem, since if you didn't have any particular place to go, which Goonie didn't, then (DUH!) what was the point of having a watch?

With the question of the correct time now relegated to the inconsequential, Goonie's mind drifted with unfettered leisure to the question of what to do once Ali arrived. This was a thorny issue, since the one time he'd broached the subject of bringing his girlfriend home for a few days had not been well-received on Javiar's part. In fact, it had been so ill-received, that Goonie's cheek had been red for a week.

So the problem was not that he couldn't bring Ali to the family apartment in Co-op City. The problem was that he'd neglected to mention this fact to Ali at any point during the planning stages of the elopement.

Goonie shook his head, feeling powerless, as he often felt when Ali was churning along. One thing was sure, she had a way of making a guy say whatever she wanted to hear. You just couldn't say no to her. She was like this huge thing, even though she barely topped five feet. She was this huge thing, and she was always rolling over you, like that big rock in *Raiders of the Lost Ark*. Who could talk to that thing? Goonie asked himself. DUH! Nobody that's who. And if that rock wanted you to do something, you did it. For a moment, Allison became precisely that talking rock in Goonie's mind.

So, Goonie, I'll stay at your place during the "elopement." Okay.

I'll eat and sleep there until my father says I can go to UCLA.

Sure.

Then, once he says I can go, you'll sprout wings and fly me to Los Angeles.

Oh, yeah, absolutely.

He shook his head and glanced at the statue of General Sheridan, reasonably sure that whatever force the general had faced, it was nothing compared to Allison Vandameer.

Roy Bumble

On the subway into the city, Roy tried to figure out where it had all gone wrong. Okay, start with lousy parents. Ted and Sheila Bumble. What a pair. Ted, who'd clearly preferred a family he could visit, rather than one he actually had to live with, had spent the lion's share of his time with his ass plastered to the fifth stool from the door at the Shamrock Fish and Rifle Club. And then there was Sheila, "The Divine Miss S," as she liked to call herself, the queen of Queens' hair salons.

Roy had never had any doubt that it was only the Catholic Church, and perhaps some vestigial fear of Hell, that had kept his parents together. If you could call it together. Mostly it had been apart. At least until they'd both ended up at the same nursing home, Ted now in his late eighties, but with a hateful clarity of mind only spite and bitterness could fully explain; Sheila utterly adrift, who, at his last visit, had stared

at Roy with blank eyes, then motioned him over, and in an urgent, conspiratorial whisper informed him that "dogs are boys and cats are girls!" What roots, Roy thought, shaking his head wearily, what great frigging roots.

The subway rattled under the East River, snaked its way westward, and finally brought Roy to his stop beneath Rockefeller Center. He still had an hour to kill before work, but the thought of hanging out on his terrace, watching Bea Bumble spill strawberry Slim-Fast on her already stain-covered housedress had been absolutely unbearable and so now here he was, under Rockefeller Center with an hour to kill before he had to step into the residential elevator at the Sherry-Netherland for eight hours of hauling its well-heeled residents up to lofty towers where no woman had ever worn a housedress and no man had ever fled his terrace under the invisible whips Roy forever felt at his back.

But forget that, Roy told himself. What was the point of hating your life if there was nothing you could do to make it better? Just concentrate on the moment, he told himself, the next sixty minutes.

Okay, so how to use that time.

There were several possibilities.

Number one, he could find a diner, take a booth in the back, order a cup of coffee, and hatch some new scheme for making the big score. The problem was that each time he'd done that in the past, the scheme had either piddled away for lack of further commitment, or suddenly gone up in smoke when he'd discovered some aspect of it that he hadn't figured on in the original plan, like the fact that ATM machines had cameras in them, for example. No, Roy thought, he was finished hatching schemes. He wanted the scheme brought to him on a silver platter like in that movie, *Oceans Eleven*, when some smart guy just calls you over for a drink and lays out the plan all thought out and decided upon, and says, "Okay, so you in or out?"

So no diner, Roy decided as he trudged up the stairs to Fifth Avenue, no schemes.

He looked at his watch again. Still a full hour to kill.

Okay, number two. He could drop in at the library. The problem here was that Roy didn't like to read.

Number three. A stroll through the museum. The problem?

They were all full of paintings and Roy had never understood what somebody got out of standing in a room, staring at some naked woman who didn't really look all that real to begin with. As a matter of fact, when the first issue of *Playboy* had hit the streets, he'd been pretty sure that most of the world's museums were doomed to close for lack of business. He was still mildly puzzled by the fact that they hadn't.

Number four. A bar. But on reflection that was no good, because Roy knew all too well that if he showed up at work with liquor on his breath, his boss, the decidedly Slavic Fydor Potanovich, would can his ass before he had time to make up a story about why he'd taken that one lousy drink; the fact, say, that his wife had died, or his poor sick mother or just some—what was the word that gay porter used for the guy he was living with in Chelsea—oh yeah, partner—had kicked the bucket and so he, Roy, had the blues, and on and on, trying to wear Potanovich down, which he couldn't do anyway, because Fydor Potanovich wouldn't give a rat's ass who died, because you didn't drink on the job . . . period.

At the top of the stairs, Roy paused long enough to be bumped forward by the people behind him.

Okay?

So?

Roy wrestled briefly with these questions.

At the end of Fifth Avenue, he could see the dark outline of Central Park. It didn't exactly beckon him, but at least the Sherry-Netherland lay in that direction. He shrugged, as if giving in to a dreary fate, then hunched his shoulders, and headed north. Maybe on the way, he thought, the answer will appear.

COGITO
ERGO SUM

Harry Stumbo

The third drink went down smoothly, but Harry felt no hint of a buzz. He'd spent too many years on the sauce for three hits to make a difference. The problem with drinking, he decided, was that it took more and more cash to get you where you wanted to go. In the old days, a couple bucks would have softened the edges, but it would take a week's salary now . . . if he actually had a salary.

"Nudder," Stumbo said.

The barkeep poured.

Stumbo knocked back the Dewar's and stared at his hangdog face in the mirror. The usual crowd was milling around, cops and firemen, construction workers who were putting up the latest luxury hotel in a neighborhood where five bucks had once bought a two-dollar whore and a three-dollar crib. Now the pensioners rented their rooms by the hour, he'd heard, though he doubted they were doing much business in the old neighborhood anymore. But worst of all, Smith's Bar was freshening up, trying for a different clientele, the old farts who arrived on charter buses and stayed down the street at the Milford Plaza, for example. Jeez, you could almost smell the Camphor Oil on those old duffers. Back when the Deuce struck at you like a pissed-off cobra, those old geezers wouldn't have dared show their faces on 45th and Eighth. Now they were everywhere. And soon, oh, heartbreakingly soon, they'd be planting their wrinkled asses on the stool right next to him and ordering—OH CHRIST!—scotch sours.

"So, Harry, how they hanging?"

The hand on Harry's shoulder and the loud voice still jangling in his ears both belonged to Chester K. Putonya, aka Cheekie Put-it-on-you, for his shameless tendency to lay the blame on someone else, but only if the guy he put the blame on was big and mean and thus certain to do Cheekie major physical harm, and thus add to Cheekie's carefully reasoned argument that little guys could only come off big if big guys regularly pounded the living crap out of them.

For his part, Cheekie had retired from the vice squad twenty years before, but still haunted the old dives of Times Square because, as the saying went, you can take the cop out of vice, but not vice out of the cop.

"So, what's up, Numbnuts?" Cheekie asked grimly, as if he were trying out the question as a provocation, a line he could burp into some huge animal's face and thus augment his reputation for taking inhuman punishment from guys three times his size.

"Nothing," Harry replied, giving far more detail than he wished.

Cheekie took a long pull on the beer he'd brought over and wiped the foam from his upper lip with a frayed, yellow sleeve. "I was talking to Jake O'Malley. He says the girls don't come in to Port Authority no more."

Harry shrugged, and Cheekie, as always, seemed to know exactly what Harry meant, which was one of the reasons Harry had taken him on as a partner, a guy to back him up.

"So, no business?" Cheekie asked.

Harry shook his head.

"Crap," Cheekie said. He took another pull on the aforementioned beer, then glanced around the bar, searching, Harry supposed, for a big guy with brass knuckles and a girlfriend he could spill the beer on.

"Work," Harry said.

"Yeah, it's a bitch," Cheekie agreed.

"Smith's," Harry added. "Change."

Cheekie set down his beer. "No crap?"

Harry nodded.

"What crap," Cheekie said. His eyes lit on Frankie Montoya, the black eyes and even blacker moustache, the rippling muscles. "I hear Frankie works for Old Man Wyatt now."

Harry shrugged, not in the least interested in the fact that Frankie Montoya, former NYPD police detective, had recently left the department to enter the glamorous world of breaking bones for the oldest shylock in New York.

"Looks like he swallowed a safe," Cheekie said.

"Big," Harry agreed.

"Or maybe just a tub full of macaroni and cheese." Cheekie smirked. "Fancy suit. All dolled up. But he's only got one ball, you know."

Harry shook his head.

"What, you think he's sensitive about that?" Cheekie blurted. "Frankie Montoya?" He laughed. "That frigging guy wouldn't feel a hatpin up his nose."

Harry cleared his throat softly.

"One ball," Cheekie mused, throwing his head back as if he were looking to gobble a little rainwater, then bringing it down again, the look in his eyes suddenly grim, and a little scary.

"Willie A-Go-Go," Harry said.

"Willie A-Go-Go," Cheekie repeated, his voice now edged in steel. "You're right. Old Man Wyatt fired Willie so's he could take Frankie on instead."

This was true, but Harry could not imagine how Cheekie could possibly have known that six weeks ago Old Man Wyatt had given Willie A-Go-Go, renowned bouncer at such equally chic meat-packer clubs as "Do Me Now" and "Pop It Hard," the most dangerous pink-slip in employment history.

"Why'd Old Man Wyatt hire Frankie?" Cheekie asked with a laugh, "Cause he's honest?"

Harry laughed, both of them aware that Frankie Montoya had been photographed by Internal Affairs so often it was a wonder he didn't have flashburn.

Cheekie sipped his beer, then wiped his mouth with the back of his hand. "I should go over to Frankie, congratulate him on the new job." He smiled. "Maybe ask if that wife of his had her long bushy tail removed yet."

Harry ducked behind the Dewar's. "Jeez," he groaned.

Roy Bumble

"Pardon me, sir, but do you have the time?"

Roy turned to the right and saw a teenaged girl with long blond hair. She was dressed to the nines, everything from Laura Ashley, a girl who looked like some kind of princess, which made perfect sense to Roy, since she was sitting no more than a few yards from General Sherman's statue, the Plaza on one corner, the Pierre only a block up Fifth Avenue, and the whole lux-

urious, filthy-rich Upper East Side a stone's throw away.

Yeah, Roy thought, a princess, or the daughter of some captain of industry, and so a girl who lived in Manhattan where he'd never be able to live because he was nothing but the captain of the residential elevator at the Sherry-Netherland.

The girl smiled sweetly. "Time?" she reminded him, as if Roy's short-term memory needed a little jog.

Roy looked at his watch. "Quarter to eight."

The girl nodded. "Thank you."

For a time Roy sat silently, merely staring at the bustling traffic. True, he thought about talking to the girl in the long skirt, but he knew it would probably scare her, even though he had no bad intentions, only the desire to talk with someone about something, just to pass the half-hour before he had to be at work. But she wouldn't believe that, Roy told himself, she'd think he was just another dirty old man. Only a few days before he'd watched a guy like that in a local bar. He must have been sixty, the poor geezer, but he just couldn't keep his eyes off this one young redhead. Finally, the redhead had spun around, nudging her brunette friend to do the same, so that the two of them stared straight at the old guy. Then the redhead said to the brunette in a voice the old duffer couldn't help but hear, "Look Angela, I see dead people."

Jeez, Roy thought, shaking his head, what a put-down. Nothing like that, he decided, would ever happen to him. So the best bet, the only course really, was to keep his eyes on the traffic and his mouth shut, and in a few minutes rise and go to work and forget about talking to some rich East Side girl he didn't know.

But she said, "That's General Sherman, the guy on the horse."

Roy looked at her. "Yeah," he said.

"He was in the Civil War. He burned everything in his path. He was the one who said, 'War is Hell.'"

"No kidding," Roy said. He briefly considered engaging the girl in further conversation, but instead returned to his original decision to keep quiet.

"You live in New York?" the girl asked.

For Roy, this was the second-worst question he could be asked. "Yeah," he said, adding nothing else.

"Manhattan?"

This was the worst question, and Roy hated the answer every time he gave it because it pegged him for a loser, a guy who'd never scored. "Queens," he muttered softly. Silence, then, "And you?"

The girl shrugged. "I don't know," she said with a short laugh.

Roy looked at her quizzically. "You don't know?" He gave her a quick once-over, figured the dress for three hundred bucks easy. "You mean, you don't know where you live?"

"Well, at least not tonight."

Roy could hardly believe his ears. If this girl was a hooker, she had the best act he'd ever seen. "Why is tonight different?" he asked.

"Because I was supposed to elope."

"Elope?"

"With my boyfriend."

Roy stared around, no boyfriend in sight. "So, where is this guy?"

She shrugged. "He was supposed to meet me here, then we were going to his place in the Bronx."

"Bronx?" Roy asked. "You were going to elope with a guy that lives in the Bronx?"

"Goonie," the girl said.

"A little bit, yeah," Roy told her.

"No, I mean, that's his name. Goonie."

"Oh," Roy said. He sucked in a quick breath. "Maybe you should just go home," he advised hesitantly.

She shook her head adamantly. "I can't."

"Why not?"

"Because, really, I wasn't going to elope."

Roy looked at her, puzzled.

"I just wanted to stick it to my dad," the girl said. She smiled and offered her hand. "Allison Vandameer," she chirped.

Roy took her hand, shook it quickly. "Roy Bumble."

The girl glanced away and stared vacantly at the Plaza.

"So . . . what now?" Roy asked cautiously.

The girl turned to him and shrugged.

"Well, you can't just sit here all night," Roy said.

The girl nodded, and Roy saw something glimmer in her eyes, the sparkle of a dark idea. "Mr. Bumble," she said. "Would you like to make some money?"

Charlie Moon

It wasn't that Charlie Moon didn't have values, Charlie reasoned as he made his way toward the Pierre, it was simply that he didn't put all that much value in them. Which was only practical after all, because values were basically suggestions. If you applied them as laws, you became rigid, or worse, self-righteous, or even worse, fanatical. And so it was a good thing, Charlie thought, that he was—the term came to him out of nowhere—"morally flexible." The fact is, adherence to values led directly to extremism. A guy who began by refusing to do a style piece might well end up bombing an abortion clinic. Charlie smiled with delight at the awesome play of his mind, its sheer and incontestable sanity.

At the Plaza he stopped and glanced about, taking in the beauty of the night. Great-looking people were coming in and out of the hotel, while others gathered around the famous fountain where F. Scott and Zelda Fitzgerald had once taken an intoxicated romp. Now those two had NO values, Charlie thought, placing himself in favorable comparison, since cutting a little slack on principle was a far cry from being a drunken fruitcake.

He moved ahead, his gait now decidedly jaunty, a sure sign that he was pleased with his reasoning. Happiness was the reward of sanity, he concluded, and being morally flexible was the soul of sanity.

The jaunty gait took him across the esplanade, and toward the glittering statue of General Sherman. To the right, the bustling traffic of Fifth Avenue, to the left the eastern border of Central Park, where he could see a few people sitting quietly, an old woman with a poodle, a young man with his cap on backwards, a young woman in a long, floral skirt, a large, pot-bellied man in a Sherry-Netherland uniform, listening intently. The varied denizens of New York, Charlie thought, as he headed across Fifth Avenue, now more secure than ever that not one of them knew what he knew about life.

DESCARTES' MANIFESTO

Arthur Vandameer

"Allison," Arthur called as he came through the door.

No answer.

Arthur stepped into the spacious living room. "Allison?"

Silence.

Down the corridor, Arthur noticed that the door to his daughter's room was slightly ajar, a phenomenon not seen in the past five years, and which suddenly filled Arthur's mind with dread.

"Allison?" He took a step toward the forbidden portal. If Allison were actually in that room, he thought, she must surely be dead. Nothing less drastic could explain the open door. "Allison?" he repeated.

Still nothing.

Arthur took a deep breath, then inched his way down the long corridor, the open door growing more ominous with each step. At the dreaded entrance, he paused, considered calling the police, or even the cook, though she was off for the night and would have to come in from the Bronx.

"Allison?" he called a final time.

When no answer came, he pressed his hand against the door and gently pushed it open. He could see Allison's bed, unmade, and those portions of the floor which were not two feet deep in teenage debris. He saw no blood anywhere, nor any sign of a body. In all aspects the room appeared abandoned, a feeling that grew more certain as Arthur's eyes fell upon a note on Allison's nightstand, a piece of stationery, or so it seemed, with an elephant at the top.

Arthur gingerly took the note and read it.

> *Deer Future Dad:*
>
> *Me and Allison are goin to get married. Because we are in love. We have been this way for a long time. We fill that we must take the nex step in hour relationship. Which is getting married to each other and no one else. We will get back in touch with you in a cupple days. Don't worry about us, she is okay. In love, like I already told you.*
>
> *Your future son-in-law*
> *Joselito Diaz that you know as Goonie*
>
> *PS: This wouldn't have happen if she could have gone to film school, but no, you said no, so she has to marry Goonie*

Arthur took a deep, trembling breath, then read the letter again.

Nothing had changed in its tone or message.

Allison had eloped. With, of all people, "Joselito Diaz That You Know As Goonie."

Arthur crumpled the letter in his shaking right hand. No, he said to himself. No, he couldn't allow Allison to ruin her life this way. Something had to be done. But what? Annulment, that's what. Allison was underage. The marriage would be void.

All right, annulment, Arthur concluded.

But that left the problem of exactly where Allison was.

She could be anywhere, Arthur thought. She could be in . . . Co-op City!

The police, Arthur decided. He would call the police. On that determination, he sprinted to the phone, yanked up the receiver and punched 9 . . . 1 . . .

But wait, Arthur thought suddenly, his mind now reverting to the consequences of such a call. If the police got involved, they would want to know certain embarrassing details. For example, they would insist on being informed as to with whom Allison had likely eloped. Which was Goonie, of course. They'd also want to know exactly why she'd taken such a step.

And what exactly would Arthur Vandameer's answer be?

He glanced at the letter again . . . and there it was.

Allison had eloped because she had an oppressive, elitist father who had repeatedly refused to entertain the idea that she go to UCLA. Arthur Vandameer, the fabled liberal television commentator, had insisted on an Ivy League school for his only daughter. He had even pulled a few discreet strings at Harvard, Yale, Princeton and Columbia, despite the fact that he'd excoriated this "affirmative action for the rich and powerful," a hundred times on his television show.

For a moment, Arthur was seized with a terrible vision, mobs of protesters outside the Pierre, placards branding him an elitist, a hypocrite, even a racist. In his mind he heard the angry throng singing "We Shall Overcome" while he was burned in effigy by Harry Belafonte, all this done to Arthur Vandameer, the only political commentator in America who'd actually voiced his support for reparations! All of it done because Allison had eloped with Joselito Diaz That You Know As Goonie.

Arthur whirled toward the window, half expecting to find Al Sharpton floating outside it, huge as a Macy's balloon, and with that dreadful accusatory stare.

Arthur's eyes widened in horror at such a prospect. "No!" he whispered.

Suddenly, the door bell rang.

Saved by the bell? Arthur dared to wonder as he headed for the door.

Charlie Moon

"Charlie Moon," Charlie Moon said, as Arthur Vandameer opened the door.

Arthur Vandameer stared at him without recognition.

"Downstairs, they sent me right up, because you'd told them to expect me," Charlie added.

The blank look on Arthur Vandameer's face did not alter.

"*Daily Register*," Charlie added. "Style Section. Jenny Cattrell couldn't make it."

The penny dropped and suddenly Arthur Vandameer's face gave off a vague sense of human awareness.

"Of course," Vandameer said shakily. "Please, come in."

Charlie stepped into the apartment. "You were expecting Jenny Cattrell, I know," he said. "But Jenny's indisposed."

Arthur Vandameer nodded briskly, then turned and led Charlie into the living room where he, Charlie, noted a vast window.

"That must be the view of Central Park," Charlie said.

"What?" Arthur Vandameer asked.

Charlie tried to decide if the great Arthur Vandameer was having a series of small strokes. "The style piece," he explained. "Views of Central Park at night."

"Oh, yes," Vandameer said. "Yes, of course." He led Charlie to the window. "This is it, as you can see."

Charlie peered out over the park's vast sweep. "Maybe you could say a few words," he said.

"Words?" Vandameer asked, blinking rapidly.

"About the view," Charlie answered.

"The view," Vandameer repeated. He lifted his hand to his lips and brushed them with a piece of crumpled paper. "To tell you the truth Mister . . ."

"Moon. Charlie Moon."

"Mr. Moon, yes," Vandameer said, "As you can probably see, I'm a bit . . . well . . . indisposed."

Charlie dropped his gaze significantly toward the paper crushed in Vandameer's fist. "Bad news?"

For a moment Vandameer hesitated, then something broke in him, and he slumped down on the sofa by the window. "My daughter. She's . . ." He stopped. "This is off the record, of course."

"Of course," Charlie said, though given the discussion he'd had with himself on the way over, he now wondered if the rule regarding off the record conversation was a journalistic law, or just a professional suggestion.

"She's eloped, evidently," Vandameer said. He handed the note to Charlie. "I don't know what to do."

Charlie opened the letter, read it, then handed it back to Vandameer, convinced that he had nothing to offer in the way of solution, until his eyes locked on the large portrait of a teenage girl that hung on the opposite wall. "That your daughter?" he asked.

Vandameer nodded.

"She's downstairs," Charlie said.

Vandameer leaped to his feet. "Downstairs?"

"Over by the Sherman statue," Charlie said. "I saw her as I was walking over."

Vandameer whirled around and rushed to the door, Charlie now racing behind him, the two of them running together through the hotel's luxurious lobby, then across Fifth Avenue, where they stood facing the statue, the empty bench to the right of it.

"Too late," Vandameer muttered despondently. He looked at Charlie. "Are you sure it was her?"

Charlie nodded. "It was her all right."

Vandameer turned back to the empty seat. "Too late," he repeated. "She's gone."

"Eloped," Charlie repeated. "With a guy you know as Goonie."

"A boy who . . . a boy . . . from . . . the Bronx."

"Riverdale?"

Vandermeer shook his head. "Co-op City."

Charlie recalled the young girl he'd seen sitting on the bench just a few minutes before. He had no doubt that it was the same girl whose portrait hung in Arthur Vandameer's apartment. And if this girl had eloped with a kid from Co-op City, then this kid was maybe a Catholic, maybe a Jew, maybe Puerto Rican, maybe even black, for Christ's sake. Holy crap, Charlie thought, no wonder Vandameer was shaking in his well-heeled boots.

"What's her name?" Charlie asked. "Your daughter."

"Allison," Vandameer answered quietly.

Allison, Charlie repeated to himself, Allison Vandameer. Perfect. A white-bread-upper-East Side-fancy-prep school-old money-"But, golly-gee, Buffy, do you really think Cornish hen is appropriate?"-name if there ever was one. And that wasn't all that was perfect about Allison Vandameer. She was just the right age to get Boy Wonder's attention. And she was from the same social class. She was a celebrity's daughter. And as if more were needed, she was damn gorgeous, which sure as hell added heat to the mix. Put it all together, then throw a little of this Bronx-Manhattan-Romeo-and-Juliet thing into the boiling brew, and, SWOOSH, Charlie could almost feel a blast of hot air shooting up his ass, lifting him up and over the jagged peaks of imminent professional ruin.

"What am I going to do?" Vandameer asked desolately.

"Don't worry," Charlie said, draping his arm over Arthur Vandameer's slumped shoulders.

Vandameer turned toward Charlie. "You'll keep this quiet, I hope?" he said tentatively.

Charlie smiled. "Absolutely," he said. Pube-scoop, he thought.

PART II

SCHOPENHAUER'S DILEMMA

THE BURDEN OF
THE INSCRUTABLE

Roy Bumble

No way, Roy thought pessimistically as the girl continued. No way could it be this good, this easy. No way could his luck change this suddenly. No way could this just fall in his lap, a Big Scam on a Major Somebody, A GUY WHO LIVES IN MANHATTAN.

Worst of all, no way could this scam work.

Or could it?

That was the question that had finally made him walk to the pay phone at the back of the TGI Friday and make the call to Fydor Potanovich, claim he was sick, then return to the back booth of the restaurant where he'd found—somewhat to his surprise—that the girl was still waiting for him.

One thing was sure, this girl—she said her name was Allison, but who the hell knew if even that much of her story was true—this girl could really be convincing. When she said her father was Arthur Vandameer, you believed her. When she said she lived in a suite at the top of the Pierre, you believed that, too. But when she said she had a boyfriend from Co-op City, whose name was Goonie Castillo de la Mancha Diaz, and who'd passed up the opportunity of eloping with her—even if it was, as she described it, a phony elopement—no way could Roy swallow that much. Not unless the afore-mentioned Goonie was even goonier than he seemed.

"He just didn't show up?" Roy asked as he slid into the booth opposite Allison Vandameer.

"You might say he just didn't get to the church on time," Allison answered cheerily. "Like the song in *My Fair Lady*," she added, "Which is really based on *Pygmalion*."

Roy didn't care about ladies or pigs at the moment. He was more interested in whether this girl had the goods, whether she could really deliver, make this thing work. If it did, he'd have an apartment in Manhattan, a lifelong dream fulfilled, though he wasn't exactly sure how he'd explain the move to Bea, unless he could make her believe that the Sherry-Netherland, in appre-ciation of his four long years of indifferent service, had given him a bonus whose exact amount he was in no position to say at the moment since the aforementioned exact amount had not yet been discussed with Allison Vandameer.

"So what would be the exact amount, do you think?" he asked. "Of the . . . reward?"

Allison appeared to think it through. "I can't give you a definite figure," she answered finally. "But a lot!"

But a lot!

The girl's eyes had all but glittered as she'd said the words. And so, Roy suspected, had his own. Still, a number would be nice, just to set things straight, as well as get a handle on just what kind of story he'd have to hand Bea. "Six figures?" he asked, hazarding an amount he hoped would not be tossed laughingly back at him.

"Oh, at least," Allison said with a wave of the hand. "Art is very, very rich. He has things people don't even know about because he doesn't want them to think he's a collector. Paintings, I mean. In the front rooms, he keeps all this stuff from Africa. Wooden masks, that sort of thing. He's always talking about how European art is elitist. But he's got a Renoir stashed in the back. Several Picassos, too. He has a Van Gogh. Also a Duchamp."

Roy didn't know Duchamp from Mike Tyson, but it sounded like Arthur Vandameer could certainly spread around some serious cash if he felt his daughter was in trouble. Of course, the guy might just hand him over one of those stupid paintings, which Roy hoped he wouldn't, since it would be hard to get rid of something like that given the fact that his friend Sal Pellucci only fenced audio equipment and car parts.

"Okay," Roy said. "Let's go over this again."

Charlie Moon

"Okay," Charlie said. "Let's go over this again."

Arthur Vandameer seemed unsure of where to begin, but Charlie decided to withhold assistance. The idea was to keep Vandameer rattled, because, as Charlie supposed, the instant he began to think clearly, the aforementioned Charlie would be out the door, because somewhere it would click that the Charlie

Moon currently seated opposite Arthur Vandameer was the same Charlie Moon who'd written half-a-dozen assaults on the very ideas Arthur Vandameer held most dear, and who—in one particular column mercifully published in an obscure and now defunct broadside— had actually called Vandameer "the Loudmouth Lefty from Looneyville."

And so for the last few minutes Charlie had sat mutely and listened, feigning tremendous sympathy, as Vandameer had carefully detailed his daughter's rela- tionship with one Joselito "Goonie" Diaz, a relation- ship that had begun, Vandameer said, in Central Park on an August afternoon when Allison and Goonie had met near the Belvedere Fountain, Allison on a school architectural assignment, Goonie thumping down the fountain's impressive staircase on a battered skate- board.

Shortly after that first encounter, Goonie had taken to visiting Allison at the Pierre, a fact made clear, according to Vandameer, by the varied array of "Goonie droppings" he'd subsequently found scattered about the apartment. These included a curiously sticky issue of *Soldier of Fortune* magazine, a half-completed applica- tion to Bob Jones University, and worst of all, or so it seemed from the exasperated look on Vandamer's face as he described it, a large political button that declared, "Three Strikes And You're Dead." "Goonie," Allison had explained pointedly, "is VERY, VERY CONSERV- ATIVE." Despite Allison's pronouncement, Vandameer was reasonably sure that Goonie had not, in fact, dropped any of these right-wing artifacts, but had merely allowed Allison to plant them about the apartment for the sole purpose of driving him, Arthur, nuts.

"Allison will do anything to upset me," Arthur said dolefully, evidently still stalled in the process of going over it again. "She secretly joined the NRA, you know. I only found out when the dues bill appeared on my American Express card."

Charlie suppressed a smile. Clearly Allison Vandameer had become fiendishly adept at sticking it to people who stuck it to her, a skill Charlie couldn't help but admire, given his own tendency to do the same. Samuel Johnson had once declared that he liked a good hater. Charlie liked a good annoyer even better. In the right hands, annoyance achieved the status of an art form, and from what he could gather, Allison Vandameer was an Olympic level ass-nipper. This was made abundantly clear by the very evidence that now faced Charlie from a distance of only a foot or two. None other than Arthur Vandameer, who appeared at that moment, incontestably, the world's most incessantly nipped ass.

"Let's start with tonight," Charlie said, at last coaxing the perennially stalled Vandameer forward.

Arthur Vandameer glanced apprehensively around the decidedly shadowy interior of the Bull and Bear, a sleek watering hole upon which imperially rested, of all things, the Waldorf-Astoria, and which he'd chosen, Charlie supposed, because it was a capitalist bastion, complete with continually rolling ticker-tape, and thus not a gin mill likely to be frequented by any of Vandameer's shaggy-haired leftist friends.

"You get home and there's this note telling you that Allison has eloped with this guy, Goonie," Charlie said. "A guy you object to, right?"

"Yes," Vandameer said quickly, then added, "But not for reasons of ethnicity or social class, of course."

"Yeah, right," Charlie said dryly. "So, anyway, this PR kid . . ."

"I'm not sure he's Puerto Rican," Arthur interrupted. "Hispanic-Americans don't like to be grouped together, you know. Any more than you'd like to be called Irish."

"I am Irish," Charlie said.

"Well, English, then."

"I'm that, too," Charlie said crisply. "May we move on?"

Vandameer looked as if he'd just been lightly scolded by his homeroom teacher. "Of course. Please continue."

"So this . . . Hispanic-American kid leaves this note," Charlie continued. He glanced toward the note that lay spread before him on the mahogany table. "And this elopement idea, you'd never heard of that before?"

"No."

"Allison had never mentioned it?"

"Never."

"Did you get the idea that she was in love with this Hispanic-American kid?"

"He could be Mexican," Arthur cautioned. "Hispanic-Americans don't like . . ."

"How about Eskimo?" Charlie barked. "For the purposes of moving on, can we say Goonie's of Eskimo extraction?"

Arthur grimaced. "To answer your prior question,

Allison never gave any suggestion that she was planning to elope with . . . this boy."

Charlie nodded. "Okay, suppose she's eloped with this Eskimo kid, what's your reaction?"

"Reaction?"

"I take it you're not pleased," Charlie said. "So, the thing is, Allison is underage. Even if she finds a way to marry this Eskimo, you could have the marriage annulled."

"I'd already thought of that," Vandameer said.

"So?"

Vandameer's eyes darkened a shade. "I'd rather not."

"Rather not what?"

"Rather not have it come to that."

"Meaning?"

Again, Vandameer glanced edgily about the room, "I'd rather not have all this come out in public. Particularly any effort to annul the marriage. The fact is, Mr. Moon, my objection to Allison's choice could easily be misconstrued."

"You mean, people might think you don't like Eskimos?" Charlie asked.

Vandameer nodded.

"Or anyone who lives in Co-op City?" Charlie added, just to press the needle in a tad further.

"The class difference might also come into play," Vandameer admitted.

"Okay, so why don't you just say that you object to the marriage because of Allison's age?"

"I can't do that either."

"Why not?"

"Because I've always said that maturity can't be judged by age. I don't think underage girls should have to inform their parents before they get abortions, for example. I'm also on the record in support of lowering the drinking age."

"Okay, suppose you say that you object to Goonie because he's, well, because he's goonie?"

Vandameer shook his head.

"What's the problem this time? The kid's dumb as a stick, right?"

"Yes, but to make such a statement might reflect upon the boy's ethnicity."

"Like saying all Eskimos are dumb?"

"Precisely."

Charlie pretended genuine sympathy for Arthur Vandameer's left-wing dilemma. "Sounds like you got your ass wedged into a pretty deep crack," he said.

Vandameer's face fell slightly. "So it would seem."

Which was, Charlie Moon realized, very good news for Charlie Moon.

"So, how can I help?" he asked sweetly.

"Perhaps . . ." Arthur Vandameer suggested tentatively, "Perhaps you could find my daughter and bring her back?" He paused, then added, "It shouldn't be that hard, should it, Mr. Moon? After all, she must be with . . ." The name of his prospective son-in-law appeared to stick in his throat. "With. . . . uh . . . Goonie."

Goonie

Once again, Goonie forgot that he didn't have a watch, and so glanced at his watch only to discover, once again, that he still didn't have a watch. Luckily, there was a rather large neon clock on a nearby storefront, one that persisted in conveying the very distressing news that Ali was very, very late.

Or was she?

Goonie couldn't be certain.

Okay, sure, Allison had said that he should meet her at the Sh-whatever-statue at seven sharp. She'd said the Sh-whatever statue was on the square, which is exactly what Javiar called the place where Goonie now waited, that is, Sheridan Square. Why the square had been named for the guy was a mystery to Goonie. But then, most of the names for squares in New York baffled him. Take for example Herald Square, which, Goonie reasoned, was probably named for General Herald. There was a statue there, but so what, Goonie concluded now, since the whole place should have been called Macy's Square anyway, since what you really noticed was not the statue of General Herald, but Macys, with that big clock, whose wide steel hands no doubt at the very moment did no more than confirm what he already knew, that Allison was really late!

"Wha choo doin' here, Joselito?"

Oh, Jeez, Goonie thought, as he glanced to the right, then up and up and up to where Javiar stood mountainously before him, not so much a person, at least to Goonie, as a tower of flaming fatherhood.

"Uh, nuttin," Goonie replied.

Javiar's moustache roused suddenly, like an angry dog. "Nuttin? Choo know wha-tine it eez, Joselito?"

As a matter of fact, Goonie did, although, when it came to Javiar's questions, he was never actually sure he had the right answer. "Eight-fifteen?"

To Goonie's surprise, Javiar did not appear all that interested in the time. "Wahchoo do here, Joselito? Choo looking for drugs, sun-ting lak det?"

"No," Goonie said, although equally uncertain that this was the correct answer, a doubt engendered by the fact that it had never seemed to matter what his answer was since Javiar never believed it anyway.

"Choo dun got no conneshun here, eh Joselito?"

Goonie shook his head.

Javiar's massive hand shot out and grabbed Goonie's already badly wrinkled shirt collar. "Choo comin wiz me," was all he said.

On the way to the subway, Goonie gave a final glance at the watch that wasn't there, then over his shoulder at General Sh-whatever. Damn, he thought, though with less distress than he'd expected, since from the grip Javiar maintained on his collar, the old man probably wouldn't have looked all that favorably on his bringing Allison home in the first place.

SINE QUA NON

Harry Stumbo

Harry Stumbo was really pissed. Of all things, Smith's Bar, the last truly sleazy gin mill on Times Square, the only one that didn't serve drinks with little umbrellas poked inside some syrupy, sickeningly sweet, probably blue liquid—THAT Smith's Bar!—was sprucing up.

Despair gathered around Harry like a thick black sheet. He knew what was coming—CHANGE—and he hated every bit of it.

First off, the damn interior lighting would change. The garish, warts-and-all lighting of Smith's would fade into the shadowy dimness of a high-end, chrome and smoked-glass adultery lounge, the type of place where middle-aged guys held hands with sleek young blonds, then escorted them upstairs to antiseptic rooms for a quick romp between cool, crisp sheets, all of it accomplished in time for the guy to catch the seven-thirty train to Scarsdale and the girl to make it back to Brooklyn Heights, where her probably gay roommate sat happily—and of course shamelessly—cruising the latest internet porn sites.

Jeez, Harry thought as he knocked back the latest round, what a world.

"Another?" Felix the Barkeep asked, the bottle of Dewar's already poised over Harry's now empty glass.

Harry nodded disconsolately.

Felix poured.

Harry drank, his gaze now drifting idly over to where Cheekie lay in semi-consciousness under a table, his face utterly blank save for the small, but incontestably triumphant smile that always swam onto his face after he'd had a good beating.

"You think Cheekie'll be okay?" Felix asked.

Harry nodded.

"So," Felix added, "How's Roxy?"

Roxy was Harry's main squeeze. Actually, she was Harry's only squeeze, and from the looks of things, she would be his last one, too. But that was okay. Roxy was just right, as far as Harry was concerned. She cooked a mean corned beef and cabbage, and after years of forgetting how much it bothered Harry, she'd finally stopped clipping her toenails in bed. Best of all, Roxy was a woman of few words. Harry had long ago accepted that this latter attribute was not due to the fact that Roxy was shy or foreign born, but only that a few words were all that Roxy knew. But so what, Harry reasoned now, as his long years with Roxy drifted through his mind, he wasn't all that much of a talker himself. As a matter of fact, he was a man of so few words, most people thought him rather clipped. Well, so what, shouldn't a gumshoe be the silent type? Alan Ladd didn't wow the girls with talk. And what about Gary

Cooper? The frigging guy hardly said a word. And besides, how much was really worth saying anyway? What hadn't already been said a thousand times? That's all people did, according to Harry, repeat themselves. So what was the point of adding to the noise? No point, Harry decided, no point at all!

Not that there wasn't a price to pay if you kept your mouth shut, never made a spectacle of yourself, blended into the woodwork.

The nature of this price had been made heartbreakingly clear to Harry by his last case, one which had plastered his ample and ever-growing behind in one of those very sleek modern lounges he'd just mentally excoriated. The old guy in question was pushing sixty, with one long white hair which he'd so artfully teased and curled that if you didn't look close, you might actually believe he had two hairs. The guy's name was Dodd, and he was a member in good standing of the City Council, and Harry had been hired by a local contractor to get something on him. Since the aforementioned Councilman Dodd was an upstanding family man, Harry had decided to investigate the most likely hypocrisy to which he would fall prey. That old standby, banging a woman other than your wife.

As it turned out, the aforementioned infidelity was in fact precisely the good Councilman's—so to speak—shortcoming. He and the woman Harry called only "The Squeeze" met once a week in the secluded, second floor bar of the Paramount Hotel on 46th Street. Harry had lolled over a scotch, watching the lovebirds for hours, the old duffer usually sucking on a scotch sour, the woman with a Brandy Alexander, both of them cooing at each other in shameless oblivion while Harry took notes and pictures . . . and a hell of a lot of umbrage.

And why the umbrage?

Because, Harry gloomily admitted as he recalled it now, Dodd and the Squeeze hadn't even NOTICED him! Harry knew, of course, that given his line of work, not being noticed was a good thing. But for some reason in this case, he'd felt positively invisible! No, worse than invisible. Irrelevant. It was as if Councilman Dodd and the Squeeze both knew damn well that it didn't really matter what Harry Stumbo saw or wrote down or even photographed, because nobody cared anymore. This change in public morality, Harry believed, was all Clinton's fault. I mean, if the president of the United States could get blown by an office bimbo and keep his job, then why the hell should anybody care what a low-watt politico like Matthew Dodd did?

Nobody, that's who, Harry thought sadly, his gaze now back on Cheekie, who was suddenly rising from the floor, swollen eyes barely open but, as Harry supposed, already searching for the next guy to ask the very question he'd posed to the imposing brute he'd located at the end of the bar a few minutes before: *So, your wife still bark at the postman?*

He knocked back the scotch, then turned away and stared at his face in the mirror. Invisible, he thought. It was a wonder he could even see himself in the glass.

He ordered a final drink, drank it down, then walked out onto Eighth Avenue, to which aforementioned Avenue Cheekie now followed him.

"Where?" Harry asked.

"Home for a while, I guess," Cheekie said. "Unless you got a better idea."

Harry shook his head.

"Okay," Cheekie said. "I'll. . . ."

Harry's cell phone rang just as a gaggle of tourists bustled past, all of them wearing green foam Statue of Liberty hats and yapping away about how great the food was at Howard Johnson's.

Harry snapped the phone from the small plastic holster that affixed it to his cracked brown belt. "Stumbo," he said, now suddenly deciding that what he needed was to hit back hard, show the whole miserable world the damage a silent, old-style man of few words gumshoe could really do.

"Harry?" the voice on the other end said, a voice Harry recognized—as if his misery weren't already deep enough—as that of Charlie Moon.

Allison Vandameer

Allison studied her newfound associate's large, somewhat puffy face. She noted the small, decidedly beady eyes, the ruddy complexion, the way the man's eyebrows painfully squeezed together each time a thought sliced through his brain.

"Well?" she asked finally.

"Go over it again," the man said.

Allison drew in and released an exasperated breath. "I pretend to have run away."

"Right."

"My father offers a reward."

"Right."

"You find me."

"Uh huh."

"You get the reward."

Allison watched as the man nodded ponderously, a gesture he'd repeated several times during their association, as if any new bit of information added a lead weight to his mind. Why this was so, Allison could not fathom, since the scheme she'd come up with more or less instantly as the two of them sat beside General Sherman hardly required a degree in rocket science to understand.

"Well?" she repeated, then waited silently as Roy Bumble nodded ponderously, and she supposed, once again slowly thought through the machinations of what he appeared to consider an infinitely complicated plot.

"So," he said at last, "It would be like a letter?"

"What?" Allison said, unable to keep the irritation from her voice.

"A letter," Roy repeated.

"Letter?" Allison snapped. "Who said anything about a letter? You call my father on the phone. You tell him you know where I am. He finds me there. You get the money."

Roy Bumble nodded ponderously.

"Sounds good, right?" Allison asked.

Roy Bumble nodded ponderously.

Jeez, Allison thought, what's the problem?

Roy Bumble

The problem, Roy decided, was Bea Bumble.

Picture this, he told himself: You go to work just like you have for the past four years, only it turns out you didn't go to work. Instead, you took a breather, met this young girl—Arthur Vandameer's daughter, Allison, no less—and lo and behold, here she is, coming through the door of Bea Bumble's apartment in Queens, where she intends to hang around until Bea Bumble's husband Roy calls Arthur Vandameer, tells him where Allison is, and then collects a six-figure sum from the grateful dad.

Sound good?

Not to Bea Bumble it wouldn't!

Because, as Roy well knew, Bea Bumble didn't have a dishonest bone in her body. Bea Bumble was the salt of the earth. Bea Bumble did not lie or steal. For all those reasons, Bea Bumble WOULD NOT go along with one damn bit of this scheme. And worse yet, if she got wind of it, Bea Bumble would kick the aforementioned Roy out on his big fat ass.

For a moment the terrible truth of this boiled around in Roy's head, a liquid that grew hotter and hotter until it finally spurted from him in the form of a desperate declaration.

"I'm married!" Roy declared desperately.

Allison looked at him quizzically.

"A wife at home is what I'm saying," Roy explained.

Allison continued to look at him, no less puzzled.

"We got to make up a story," Roy continued. "About . . . how we hooked up."

"Hooked up?" Allison asked, the quizzical look now so deeply ingrained in her face, Roy was pretty sure it was permanent.

"Met," Roy said. "Out of the blue, I mean. Got together. The whole . . . you know . . . story."

"And this is necessary . . . .why?" Allison asked.

"So you can stay at my place," Roy told her. "You know, with my wife Bea. Until we pull this thing off."

"Stay at your place?" Allison asked. "I was thinking of a hotel."

"Hotel?" Roy said. "You'd have to register. People would see you. Suppose your father goes to the TV people, gives interviews. Your face would be everywhere." He could see that this was a circumstance Allison did not appropriately dread. "It would spoil the deal," he added emphatically.

"Yes," Allison said, though with obvious reluctance, like Miss America handing over her crown. "Right."

"Okay," Roy said, his brain now whizzing along, relentlessly working up a tale. "Okay, how about this? You came up to me on the street. You was mugged in the park. You didn't have no money, no place to stay." He smiled. "Yeah, that's it. Your folks kicked you out, and you didn't have no place to stay."

"Sooooo . . . ?" Allison inquired, clearly seeking the further development of the story.

"So . . . I . . . took you . . . in?"

He could see that Allison was turning this over in her mind.

"Took me in," she said quietly. "Until I can . . . ?"

"Get on your feet?" Roy hazarded.

"In my . . . profession?"

"Yeah, okay, your profession."

"Which is . . . filmmaker?"

"Sure, okay," Roy said, now as happily convinced that the whole thing would work as he'd previously been happily convinced that Speed Trap would come home first in the Trifecta.

Allison smiled.

Roy smiled.

Roy put out his hand.

Allison shook it.

"Partners in crime," Roy said.

E PLURIBUS UNUM

Arthur Vandameer

Arthur simply knew no other place to go, and so he went there, his long, mournful face even longer and more mournful when Madelyn answered the door.

He'd left Charlie Moon at the corner of Park and 50th only a few minutes before, then strode uptown, intent on returning to the Pierre, when he'd suddenly found himself on Madelyn's block, her townhouse a mere few yards away, the light burning bright with its promise of . . . what?

Arthur wasn't sure. But it certainly wasn't sympathy, since Madelyn's cup never ran over with that particular form of fellow-feeling. As a matter of fact, he'd long ago noticed that Madelyn never failed to lay the blame for any particular human fate precisely at the feet of the particular person whose fate it particularly was. When Harrison Bellows drowned, well, jeez, what was he doing in water that was over his head anyway? When Gloria Whitmason died in a plane crash, well jeez, what did she expect, sitting there, sipping a double martini at thirty-three thousand feet? Madelyn, of course, neither swam nor flew. Neither did she walk more than half a block on a city sidewalk. Thus when Heather Banks was hit by a bus at Madison and 51st, Madelyn characteristically lay the blame squarely where it belonged. *Well, jeez, what did Heather expect, standing on the street?*

Madelyn similarly withheld sympathy for life's less disastrous eventualities.

If people got divorced, for example, well jeez, what did they expect after getting married? If their kids went bad, well, jeez, what did they expect, having kids? If they went bankrupt, well, jeez, what did they expect, putting their money in businesses, stocks, pork belly futures?

Madelyn, for her part, placed every cent of her own substantial liquidity in solid, guaranteed, interest-bearing accounts whose numbers, Arthur supposed, were known only to herself and her mean-faced little Pekinese, neither of whom, quite clearly, was inclined to divulge them. That none of these funds had ever actually been earned by the aforementioned Madelyn through the personal exercise of actual human labor made no impression on her otherwise impressive clarity of mind, a fact that Arthur could not with equanimity bring up, however, since the lion's share of his own tidy empire had been similarly acquired, that is, through the timely deaths of well-heeled relatives.

And so, Arthur went straight to another, less vulnerable point. "Allison has eloped," he said.

Madelyn, who, rather oddly to Arthur's mind, was no longer clothed in the red silk kimono in which she had been so luxuriously wrapped when last they'd been together, eyed him with a wholly predictable lack of sympathy.

"Well, jeez, Arthur, what do you expect, having a teenaged daughter?"

"Not all teenage daughters elope, Madelyn," Arthur reminded her. "My point being that Allison, specifically, has eloped."

Madelyn remained unmoved, as well as unsympathetic. "Well, what do you expect, Arthur, after the way you raised her?"

"What way is that, if you don't mind my asking?" Arthur asked.

"Without boundaries," Madelyn replied.

Arthur could not help but be offended. "Allison had boundaries," he said.

"And you were always in her face, Arthur."

This was an expression Madelyn had never used, but she'd come to it so readily Arthur had no doubt that it had long been her opinion that as a father, he—to use another street-phrase—sucked.

"May I come in?" Arthur asked, his eyes now in full imitation of a homeless spaniel.

Madelyn noticeably stiffened, body language which, in Arthur's mind, immediately explained the otherwise unexplainable absence of a red kimono.

"I see," he said, now eyeing a curiously familiar large white cowboy hat that hung with alarming casualness on the brass hat rack just inside Madelyn's door. "Is Roland . . . ?"

Madelyn, of course, did not give an inch. "Well, jeez, what did you expect, Arthur?" she asked with a pointed glance below the waist which, as Arthur immediately surmised, constituted a less than subtle comment on his earlier performance.

"Is that really all I am to you?" Arthur asked brokenly.

"If you were that, then you'd be that," Madelyn explained crisply, "But since you're not, you're not."

Arthur stared at her blankly, his mind working to untwist the rather knotty answer Madelyn had just offered.

He was still parsing the sentence when Madelyn added, "Goodnight, Arthur," then unceremoniously closed the door, leaving the aforementioned Arthur decidedly at a loss for further consolation.

"Well all right, then," Arthur muttered huffily in a brief effort at actual manliness before the inevitably deflating follow-up question arose: *Well, all right then. . . . what?*

Charlie Moon

Charlie ordered a shot of rye and waited. He had no doubt that Harry Stumbo would show up. The only question was his mood. Which really wasn't a question at all, as Charlie now reminded himself, since Harry Stumbo's mood was always gloomy.

He even looked faintly gray, Charlie noticed, as Harry stepped through the door of the Times Square Bar, a 9th Avenue dive where they'd often met in the past, a place with sawdust on the floor and a shadowy line of booths in the back. The only trouble with the

place, so Harry Stumbo had mentioned the last time they'd met, was that Harry had seen kids coming out of the place the preceding Halloween. Kids, for Christ's sake, AT THE TIMES SQUARE BAR.

And so, to make the site more congenial to Harry's vision of the way things should be, Charlie had purposely picked the darkest booth he could find, the one at the very back, near the bathroom. He was reasonably sure that the smell of stale urine that wafted from it each time the door opened would help provide the healthy atmosphere Harry preferred.

"Charlie," Harry said morosely as he lumbered over and lowered himself into the booth.

"Harry," Charlie said with a quick nod.

"So?" Harry asked.

"I got a job for you. It involves a pretty big fish. Arthur Vandameer. The pinko television commentator. Never met a cop killer he didn't like. THAT Arthur Vandameer."

"Problem?"

"His daughter took a hike."

"Age?"

"Seventeen."

"When?"

"A few hours ago."

"Why?"

"Seems she eloped with a kid from the Bronx. Some PR from Co-op City. One Joselito Castillo de la Mancha Diaz. Called Goonie."

"Job?"

"I want you to find the girl. But when you find her, don't tell anybody but me. This whole thing is very hush-hush, you know, what with Vandameer being such a big fish and all."

"Okay."

"Good."

Harry picked up his hat. "Charlie."

Charlie nodded. "Harry."

Now why the hell, Charlie wondered as Harry lumbered back out the door, couldn't Congress work like that?

NEVER PUT DESCARTES BEFORE THE HORSE

Allison Vandameer

Roy watched silently as Allison stared at the dark, gaping mouth and shuddered.

"Subway?" she asked incredulously. "We're going on the subway?"

"Well . . . yeah," Roy said.

Allison returned her gaze to the subway entrance. "But it's UNDERGROUND."

"Well . . . yeah."

Clearly Allison did not find Roy's response in any way responsive. "Can't we call a service?" she asked.

Roy Bumble took this request for what it surely was, a capital expenditure he could not afford. "That would cost fifty, sixty bucks," he explained. When this had no effect, he added, "Maybe more."

Allison gave a quick sigh, then waved her hand. "All right, let's go," she said, the crinkle turning into a vaguely sour expression, so that as they headed down the stairs, Roy half expected her to pinch her nose.

On the ride to Queens, Roy felt every bump and swerve, heard each loud grinding of the brakes, the high squeal of the tracks, and knew, absolutely knew, that of all the unprofitable schemes in which he had ever been involved, this one—with this girl—was the worst.

I mean, he thought, mixing mathematical metaphors, the numbers added up to a fixed equation: 1 Rich Girl + 1 Rich Father = 1 Roy Bumble Taking the Fall.

The horrible specter of Patricia Hearst rose to the forefront of Roy's increasingly worried mind. Here she was, a rich girl who gets kidnapped by some psychos, ends up robbing a bank, and before you know it, she's doing commentary on cable. But where are the psychos? Frigging dead, that's where. Burned to a crisp, for God's sake. In a terrible, visionary moment, Roy saw himself sitting like a monk, his body barely visible in the swirling flames. At least the monk had been a martyr for something. What was Roy Bumble a martyr for, Roy Bumble asked himself. BEING STUPID THAT'S WHAT!

"Crap," Roy hissed under his breath.

Allison's eyes slid over to him. "I'm hungry," she said, with an oddly tense squirming motion whose exact meaning Roy could not fathom. "Can we go out to eat?"

Charlie Moon

Charlie Moon watched the gleaming nightbound traffic of Manhattan with a feeling of solid invincibility. This was not exactly a new feeling, as Charlie knew, only this time there was an actual reason for it.

And that reason was the pube-scoop. Particularly its double-edged quality, the fact that he could nail down an exclusive while at the same time exposing Arthur Vandameer for the limousine lefty he so clearly was.

Jeez, Charlie exulted, what a break.

As he headed down 42nd Street, bound for the imposing offices of *The New York Register*, Charlie gleefully reviewed the plot points:

1) Allison Vandameer had eloped.
2) Arthur Vandameer wanted her back.
3) Charlie was going to get her back.
4) Charlie would get the exclusive, a pube-scoop to die for, his stock with Boy Wonder suddenly vaulting to an all-time high.
5) The exclusive would nail the aforementioned Arthur Vandameer to the proverbial church house door.

True, when tied together Parts 4 and 5 were not without ethical ambiguity, given the fact that Charlie had promised Vandameer that the whole affair would be kept strictly off-the-record. But what was the use of professional ethics, Charlie wisely reasoned, if they got in the way of getting a story? From this premise, others followed like soldiers in a line. If you didn't get the story, there'd be no story to print. If there were no stories to print there'd be no newspapers. And if there were no newspapers, there would be no advertising. If there were no advertising, people wouldn't buy things they didn't need at prices they couldn't afford, and the nation's economic underpinnings would be shaken. If the nation's economic underpinnings were shaken, the Republic itself might fall prey to left-wing extremists. Hence, Charlie concluded, it had been nothing less than his patriotic duty to lie his head off to Arthur Vandameer.

Thus swelled with pride and impulsively whistling a rousing version of the "Battle Hymn of the Republic," Charlie stepped into Boy Wonder's office a few minutes later.

"Charles," Boy Wonder said, clearly surprised to see Charlie smiling happily at the threshold. "You seem in somewhat . . . martial spirits."

Charlie's smile broadened. "Jenny still indisposed?"

"Yes, she is," Boy Wonder replied, now looking a bit suspicious.

Clearly, as Charlie saw, a happy Charlie Moon did not in and of itself a happy Boy Wonder make, which made Charlie even happier, since, from the look on Boy Wonder's face, the aforementioned Boy Wonder was not entirely confident that good news was in the offing.

Charlie's smile broadened yet again, so that it now pretty much covered the entire lower third of his face. "Arthur Vandameer's daughter is missing," he sang cheerily. "Vanished." He laughed and slapped his hands together gleefully. "Frigging kid didn't leave so much as a puff of blue smoke behind her."

Boy Wonder looked perplexed. "Vanished? Allison Vandameer?"

"You know the kid?" Charlie asked.

"Faintly," Boy Wonder answered. "And why," he

asked, "is Allison's disappearance a source of your, shall we say, paramilitary mirth?"

"Because I've got an exclusive, that's why," Charlie replied. "Nobody but me even knows the kid's missing. So the whole story, from beginning to end, is strictly for the *Register*." His smile now covered fifty percent of his face. "And it's a story that's got everything." He lifted his hand, using one finger at a time to illustrate each respective point. "One, you got a great-looking teenaged girl. Two, she's a celebrity's daughter. Three, she's missing. Four, I'm gonna find her. Five, I'm gonna bring her back to her loving father . . . the celebrity. Six, Toots McTeague will be there to take a picture of the much-sought reunion. Seven, that picture will be on the front page of the *Register*." He stopped, reluctant to state out loud what would clearly be point eight: *Charlie Moon will be the most famous reporter in New York for a good deal longer than the fabled fifteen minutes.*

"It's all in the bag, know what I mean?" Charlie asked.

Boy Wonder didn't. "What makes you think you can find Allison Vandameer?"

"Cause she couldn't have gone far," Charlie replied confidently. "Ran off with this dumbass PR from Co-op City. So how far could she go? My guess? Co-op City." He laughed. "I got the kid's name, and as of ten minutes ago, I got a guy to do the job."

"A guy?" Boy Wonder asked.

"A personal friend," Charlie said.

"And this . . . fellow . . . where is he now?"

Charlie's smile now covered eighty-five percent of

his face. "My guess? At the no doubt graffiti-encrusted apartment house of one Joselito Castillo de La Mancha Diaz," he said. "Affectionately known as Goonie."

Boy Wonder leaned forward. "Charles, did you introduce yourself to Arthur Vandameer?"

"Sure," Charlie said, though now beginning to see a dark cloud on the horizon.

"You gave him your full name?"

"I think so."

"And he gave you an exclusive. You. Charles W. Moon?"

"Yeah," Charlie said.

Boy Wonder appeared genuinely baffled. "It isn't possible."

"What's the problem?" Charlie asked

"The problem, Charles, is that Arthur Vandameer would never trust you."

"Why not?"

"Because you are, among other things, somewhat to the right of Vladamir the Impaler. Arthur Vandameer would have to realize that any story you wrote about him would be deeply prejudiced."

"Sure," Charlie said, "But so far I've kept him in the dark about me."

"Meaning?"

"He doesn't know I'm THAT Charlie Moon," Charlie said. "In the dark, like I said, about that."

"But dawn will soon break, Charles," Boy Wonder said with alarming confidence. "And the only reason it hasn't broken already is probably because Vandameer is upset, and so not thinking clearly. But believe me,

Charles, you are one sudden, shocking realization away from having this so-called exclusive snatched from your hands."

"And given to whom?"

"A reporter Arthur Vandameer can trust."

Charlie's eyes widened in horror. "Jenny? Jenny Cattrell?" he sputtered.

"But she didn't . . . she wouldn't . . ."

"One sudden realization," Boy Wonder repeated. "Then a phone call." He glanced at his watch. "I'm rather surprised Arthur Vandameer hasn't made it yet."

Harry Stumbo

Harry Stumbo stared at the graffiti encrusted apartment house he'd once lived in, then out over the sprawling lanes of I-95, to the scrubbed, but profoundly charmless towers of Co-op City.

He hadn't been in his old neighborhood for more than twelve years, and that had only been briefly, for his mother's funeral. At the funeral he'd made not the slightest effort to appear in the least concerned that his last living relative was, in fact, no longer living. "Bitch," he'd explained when Roxy had commented upon his all too apparent indifference to his mother's demise.

Once at Co-op City, Harry lumbered from building to building, until he located a group of kids who appeared to be the proximate age of the young man in question.

"Hey," Harry asked to the group in general. "Know a kid named Goonie?"

"Goonie?" one of the boys said, "Yeah, they's a kid named Goonie lives here."

"Puerto Rican?" Harry asked.

The kid nodded. "Yeah, I guess."

"Your age?"

"Yeah."

"Live alone?"

"Nah, he lives with his family. Father's named Javiar. Big frigging guy."

Harry nodded coolly, despite the small line of sweat that had instantly appeared on his brow, walked to the pay phone outside the building and dialed the number.

"Cheekie, here," the voice said on the other end.

SPINOZA'S MONAD PROBLEM

Arthur Vandameer

Arthur Vandameer considered his earlier options. None of them appeared any more acceptable than at the instant he'd rejected them.

He could not physically pursue Allison, and once found, physically make her return to the Pierre because such an action smacked not only of parental authoritarianism, but of vigilantism, as well, a mob activity he had repeatedly condemned in his television commentary.

He could not find Allison, speak with Goonie or any of his surrogates, and offer a generous financial remuneration should she be returned to him, because it would be seen as a rich man buying himself out of a problem, and he could easily imagine a full history of this sort of thing, complete with pictures of, for example, a drenched Ted Kennedy lumbering away from the bridge at Chappaquidick.

He could not give the slightest hint that Goonie was, himself, unworthy of Allison, since Goonie was, himself, the depository of innumerable protected identities, not only a doubtlessly deprived "oirbun yoot," as the average

New York City cop would have called him, but one of Hispanic, working-class descent.

All of these options had raced through Arthur's tormented mind before he'd finally dismissed each in turn and thus embarked upon a separate course.

For a moment, he saw Charlie Moon once again standing in his spacious living room, eyeing the portrait of Allison with a curiously satisfied look on his face. If Charlie had been a dog, he'd have surely wagged his tail at that moment.

Charlie Moon!

The name suddenly flamed up in Arthur's head. Wasn't Charlie Moon the dread, politically incorrect gadfly who, some years before, had written a small book called *The Sane Guy's Guide to Life*? A book in which, among other things, the aforementioned Moon had proposed arming teenaged girls, renaming lotto tickets so that customers would have to call out "Give me three Dumb Asses and one Stupid Crap," rather than three Gold Nuggets and one Super Cash; and opposed the death penalty only because "the current methods are way too fast."

Yes, Arthur realized with sudden horror, it was THAT Charlie Moon, the one who'd laughingly advocated an affirmative action program for the NBA; "runt quotas" for the vertically challenged; a man who'd loudly advocated handicap buses "but only when equipped with catapults."

Arthur slapped his head in stricken disbelief. Yes, undoubtedly, it was THAT Charlie Moon, a man who stood grimly in the way of every enlightened impulse; THAT Charlie Moon, to whom he, Arthur, had unwittingly delivered himself; THAT Charlie Moon—oh, the horror, the horror—with whom, and without doubt, he was now in league.

Arthur's eyes darted toward the liquor cabinet where lay carefully sequestered his last bottle of Dow 63. Time for a drink, he thought.

Roy Bumble

Roy paused at the door of his apartment, turned to Allison, and decided that they should go over it just one more time. "Okay, I was just sitting there at the Plaza, having a smoke—no, not a smoke—having . . . having nothing, just sitting, and so you come up all teary, and lost and crap like that, and you tell me about how you got mugged, and this job you have is. . . ."

"I'm a filmmaker," Allison reminded Roy.

"Right, filmmaker," Roy said. "Anyway. You need a place to stay . . . just for a couple nights until your, job . . ."

"Until the shoot starts," Allison said insistently. "It's a movie about a young filmmaker's search for creative identity."

"Yeah, right," Roy said.

"A search for fulfillment."

"Uh huh."

"Told from several different artistic perspectives."

"Whatever you say."

"With each character represented by a different camera angle."

Roy nodded. "Anyway, you need a place to stay until this movie . . ."

"Shoot."

". . . starts."

Allison released an exasperated breath. "Precisely."

A problem occurred to Roy, and, as usual at such moments, his face drew into a kind of fleshy crinkle. "Uh . . . how long?"

"An independent film needs to run two hours if it has any hope for commercial distribution," Allison said.

"No, I mean, how long til this . . . shoot . . . starts."

Allison considered the matter. "Let's say, a week."

"That long?" Roy asked.

"Well, we have to communicate with my father. He has to mull it over. And he mulls a long time. He's sort of a muller."

"But . . . a week?"

"A week, yes," Allison repeated, her eyes squeezing together in that stern there-will-be-no-further-discussion-of-the-matter way that Roy had, by then, come all too well to recognize.

"Okay," he said, then turned back to the door, and took a deep, tremulous breath, as the image of a piercingly suspicious Bea Bumble reared before him like a dragon at the entrance of a cave.

Harry Stumbo

When Cheekie Putonya arrived, Harry took the time to fill him in on the situation.

"Girl."

"Yeah?"

"Eloped."

"Okay."

"Father's big."

"Okay."

"Three hundred."

"If?"

"Back home."

"Okay."

The two men nodded somberly, then turned and headed back into the building, Harry feeling curiously exhausted by such a lengthy explanation.

Charlie Moon

When the phone rang, Charlie shivered. Before his little talk with Boy Wonder, he'd have snatched it up jauntily, as if expecting to hear Vicky, his old lover, now eight years dead, telling him how great he was in bed.

Such WOULD HAVE BEEN the mood of Charlie Moon. But Boy Wonder had killed it, turned the phone into a coiled snake, one he now gingerly picked up.

"Uh, hello . . . "

"Hello, Mr. Moon?"

Crap, Charlie thought as he instantly recognized the unwelcome voice of Arthur Vandameer. "Moon?" he asked with a happy chuckle. "As in 'Over Miami'"?

"It's Arthur Vandameer."

"As in *For the Misbegotten*?" Charlie sang, now feeling that he'd hit upon a tactic that might yet save him. It was simple. He would act like a lunatic.

"Uh . . . well . . . given the . . ."

"Sure, sure," Charlie sang. "But those dark clouds will soon disperse."

"Well . . ."

"Disperse and be gone!" Charlie cried with mock Shakespearean pomp, as if he were crying havoc to let slip the dogs of war.

"Well . . ."

"The ends of the earth, my dear man," Charlie said with sudden somberness, his mood now melodramatically plunging into a dark and dreary gloom. "You may seek to the ends of the earth and still not find it."

"What?"

"Youth must be restrained."

"Uh."

"Not tethered, mind you," Charlie cautioned, "Not disciplined with too long a martingale."

"Martingale?"

"Riding crop," Charlie explained.

"Well . . . no . . . but . . . is this Mr. Moon?"

"Woops," Charlie yelped with a quick glance at his watch. "You'll have to forgive my abrupt departure. I have a date with destiny." He giggled hysterically. "Actually, it's Vicky, and she's got a rack like a leg of lamb." He threw back his head and cackled madly.

"But. . . ."

"Tah tah," Charie cried, then hung up.

Okay, he thought breathlessly as he leaped to his feet and stormed away from the phone, leaving it jangling once again as he closed the door behind him, *Okay, in what direction does true wisdom lie?*

Harry Stumbo

The minute the door of Goonie Castillo de La Mancha Diaz's apartment opened, Harry knew he was in deep trouble.

It wasn't that Javiar Esperanza Gomez was just big. It wasn't that he was mountainous. It was that he looked like a huge pile of stones. Everything about him was oversized. His arms hung like great slabs of beef, at the end of which hands the size of pizzas all but touched the floor. His eyes, black and murderous, were dark wells into which city buses could easily disappear. His moustache was stretched like a king-sized comforter across a mouth that could, Harry supposed, take a large bite out of Yonkers.

But there was a problem even more serious, Harry realized, and that was the fact that one look at this guy, and all hope of negotiation would fly out the window, because Cheekie would absolutely have to have a beating. This was unavoidable, as Harry well knew, because Cheekie weighed things according to a system of weights and measures that was strictly Cheekie's. According to this system, you rated big guys by the size of their bodies, and little guys by the size of their balls.

The rudimentary logic of this system decreed that Cheekie Putonya wouldn't give a flying taco how big Javiar Esperanza Gomez was. In fact, for Cheekie, the bigger the better. Because the bigger Javiar's body was, the more fully Cheekie could display his incontestably enormous testicles.

Put these two factors together, Harry realized, and it

was highly probable that nobody was going get out of this thing alive.

"Chess?" Javiar asked darkly, shifting his gaze from Harry to Cheekie, then back to Harry. "You wahn sumping?"

"Stumbo," Harry explained with a lame smile, "Joselito . . ."

"Goonie," Cheekie cackled. "You got a kid with a stupid ass name like that?"

"Stoopie-hasss?" Javiar said grimly. He looked at Harry. "Who deez guy?"

"I'm Harry's bitch," Cheekie blurted with a sneering grin.

Javiar's eyes swept over to Cheekie like two battle-ship howitzers. "Beech?"

Cheekie laughed.

"Wazso funny?" Javiar demanded. "Mebbe I steek my foot up you ass. Mebbe that may me laugh."

"Laugh? Really?" Cheekie said, "I figured it would just give you a hard-on."

"Jeez," Harry moaned.

But it was too late. Cheekie was already rolling head over heels down the long corridor, Javiar bounding after him, his enormous frame pounding thunderously from wall to wall as he tossed Cheekie right and left as if he were no more than a large pink beach ball.

When it finally stopped, Javiar snorted like a spent bull, then headed back up the corridor, leaving Cheekie on his back, unconscious, but with a psycho smile on his face.

"You wahn sum?" Javiar demanded grimly.

Harry shook his head.

"Choo go way now," Javiar commanded.

Harry nodded.

"Choo dun cum beck, choo unnerstan?."

"Understood," Harry promised.

With that, Javiar retired like a vast tidal wave into the inner sanctum of Apartment 27-A, leaving Harry to clean up the puddled remains of Cheekie Putonya, whose stringy frame, once heaved over Harry's shoulder, was surprisingly light, given Cheekie's dead-weight condition.

Once back in his car, Harry slapped Cheekie's pale white face a couple of times, thus returning the aforementioned Cheekie to whatever height of consciousness he'd been able to attain before Javiar had wadded him up like a spit-ball and hurled him against whatever wall the aforementioned Javiar found sufficiently sturdy for a splatter test.

"Okay?" Harry said with heartfelt condolence.

"Yeah," Cheekie responded, his eyes sparkling with pride in a job well done. "Guess I showed that asshole you don't screw around with Cheekie Putonya."

"Big," Harry agreed.

"A frigging freight train," Cheekie said, lifting one hand in triumph, the white teeth of a smile now showing through the otherwise purplish folds of the aforementioned Cheekie's considerably reconstituted facial features.

"Teeth," Harry said, locked in wonder at the fact that any of them remained in Cheekie's head.

"Oh, yeah," Cheekie answered proudly. "A guy like

that, I always slip in a mouthpiece before the action starts." The grin now radiated the vast extent of Cheekie's accomplishment. "Fool the bastards every time."

"Goonie," Harry said.

Cheekie waved his hand. "Oh, don't worry; we'll just sit here 'til the little weasel comes out. Then we'll nail him."

"Javiar," Harry reminded him.

"Screw Javiar," Cheekie said with a sly smile. "Bouncing me around like that, he's gotta be worn out."

THALES' WATER PROBLEM

Allison Vandameer

Allison had no idea that an apartment could actually LOOK like this. Sure, she'd seen a few similar places flash by as she surfed toward MTV; or when Art wasn't around, the History Channel. But that such apartments actually existed, this was news, and so she took a moment to survey her current accommodations.

First there was the sofa covered in a thick clear plastic. On either side of the sofa stood two towering lamps that dripped enormous glass baubles that were themselves framed in a mock gold leaf. Above the sofa there was a painting Allison recognized as Gainsborough's "Blue Boy," the portrait overwhelmed by a huge rectangular frame that also sported a considerable amount of gold leaf. In front of the sofa, there was a wooden table with a pink marble top. It was oval shaped, and its entire surface was covered with small porcelain figurines that seemed to be modeled after the peasants Allison had once glimpsed in a pictorial history of feudalism. They were all smiling, despite their ragged clothes, an attitude Allison found difficult to imagine, since as far as she could see, poverty was a drag.

Things did not get any better as Allison continued
to survey the room. For despite the fact that one corner of the cramped living room was stacked with
unopened boxes of audio equipment, a tower that rose
almost to the ceiling, the actual entertainment center of
the Bumble residence remained decidedly retro. There
was a boxy old television which looked oddly naked
without accompanying DVD player and Home Video
Speakers; a wooden cabinet the size of a casket, which
contained a dusty turntable and gigantic plastic knobs
but which, for all its space-devouring size, gave no sign
of either tape or CD player; and finally a small wooden
shelf where two chrome rabbit ears soared nearly to the
low-slung, and weirdly sparkling, ceiling—this last
contraption the most compelling evidence yet, as
Allison saw it, that she'd somehow entered The Land
That Time Forgot.

"You like Mantovani?"

Allison drew her gaze from the Time Capsule
Home Entertainment Center to the large, curiously
woolen recliner in which Bea Bumble presently
reclined.

"What?" Allison inquired softly.

"Mantovani," Bea Bumble repeated.

Allison was reasonably certain that Mantovani must
be some type of pasta.

"Mantovani and Mancini," Bea Bumble added.
"Those are my favorites."

Allison resisted the impulse to inquire as to whether
Mrs. Bumble preferred these delicacies with white or
red sauce.

Bea Bumble shifted slightly beneath the thickly bundled housedress that made her look as if she were being hugged to death by a headless old woman.

"So," she said, one eye glinting slightly, "You just ran into Roy, eh?"

Allison realized suddenly that the small talk about pasta had been only a ruse, a way of softening her up for the brutal interrogation that was surely to come. Bea Bumble had shrewdly waited until Roy had retired to the bathroom for what now seemed an interminable period of . . . whatever he was doing in there . . . and was now coming in for the kill, just as the aforementioned Roy had warned.

"Yes," Allison said sweetly. "It was really nice of him to . . . help me."

"Nice," Bea Bumble said coolly, the furry brown eyebrow now arching over her still glinting eye.

Allison had never been gone over by anyone like this, she realized as Bea Bumble continued to gaze at her with all the lethal intensity of a coiled rattler. Sure, she'd seen a few guys mentally undress her. And the way Wendy Jamison, her school's somewhat mannish volleyball coach, looked at her had a way of making you keep a tight grip on your towel before you stepped out of the shower. But Bea Bumble's gaze did more than peel off your clothes. It took a bite out of you. That was it, Allison realized with a shiver, Bee Bumble's eyes were LIKE FANGS!

"So," Bea Bumble said, her voice slithering from her mouth with all the welcoming warmth of a forked tongue. "So, you and Roy just met up in the city, eh?"

Arthur Vandameer

Arthur Vandameer closed the novel he'd hoped might divert his increasingly feverish attention from the growing certainty that one Charles W. Moon was out to get him. As for the book, he hadn't liked it anyway. All that straining to be deep and philosophical. He'd been particularly annoyed by the fact that the chapter titles, often weighted with the names of prominent European philosophers or written in Latin or other foreign languages, made no sense, but that was typical of the modern novel, he groused, anything to pump up the volume, make you think the writer was just soooo clever, when really all he had going for him was youth, which Arthur did not have, vigor, which he also lacked, and a cynical view of mankind supported by nothing more than the flimsy evidence of all human history.

Damn, Arthur thought as he laid the book on the Italian marble pedestal beside his bed. For a moment he peered about his bedroom. Its décor had been chosen by his first wife, a budding Marxist scholar from Yale whose Ph.D. thesis on Mexican peasant rebellions had won Arthur over to the cause of Emilio Zapata even before he'd seen Marlon Brando in the movie. Deidre, who'd changed her name to Della because, she said, "it sounded more black," had spent most of her youth stapling placards to wooden sticks while her schoolteacher parents made pro-Communist speeches at Union Square. The problem was that Deidre-Della had scarcely had a single proletarian impulse that had not been stuffed down her throat from the time she'd first been swaddled in a red diaper. In fact, as Arthur quickly discovered after the marriage, the only thing red about Deidre-Della was the usual number of corpuscles. As for the rest, Deidre-Della was about as progressive as Cornelius Vanderbilt, and once married to Arthur, to whom she soon attached the affectionate sobriquet "Money Bags," Deidre-Della had gone on a buying spree that had lifted the voice of Bloomingdales in song.

The bedroom about which Arthur now dismally cast his gaze was, in part, the result of that fabled bacchanal. Everything marble and satin, the bath in the adjoining room fashioned from white onyx, the toilet bowl itself a work of art with fluttery, scalloped sides that made it look as if it at any moment it might actually take flight.

Predictably, the divorce that swiftly followed Deidre-Della's descent into a mindless, but very expensive, materialism had been anything but amicable, with Deidre demanding eighty percent of everything Arthur had, except—and this she'd actually said in an otherwise colorless attempt at arbitration—"his little acorn of a dick."

Jeez, Arthur thought, now desperately trying to drive the incident from his mind, *I'd rather think about Charlie Moon.*

Which he immediately began to do.

But what could he do about this man?

That was the question.

And in the frantic way in which Arthur thought about everything, that is, with the whip of an unspecified panic forever at his back, Arthur, well, began to think.

Charlie Moon, he ruminated, stroking his beardless chin, *Charlie Moon*.

Further than this, as he discovered an hour later, he was not able to go.

Harry Stumbo

From his place behind the serrated plastic steering wheel of his 1994 Dodge Dart, Harry Stumbo recognized the young man he'd earlier glimpsed just beyond the monumental figure of Javiar Esperanza Gomez at the entrance of Apartment 27-A.

"Goonie," he muttered

Cheekie seemed to emerge from a dense, interior fog. "Prick."

"Talk."

"Yeah, but suppose he won't give up the girl?"

"Try," Harry commanded.

"Yeah, all right," Cheekie muttered, clearly disappointed that further physical harm to himself might actually be averted.

By then Goonie had stepped into that shadowy darkness that perpetually enshrouds the otherwise delightfully phantasmagorical atmosphere of Co-op City.

"Go," Harry said as he jerked open the door.

Cheekie immediately did the same, the two men now moving rapidly toward Joselito Castillo de la Mancha Diaz, otherwise known as Goonie, their footsteps echoing in the blackness, loud as horses' hooves as they closed in, so loud and charged with evil mission in fact, that

Goonie, thus alerted, glanced back, then, his eyes now large as garbage lids, took off for . . . what?

Harry couldn't imagine, since Co-op City, with its high, flat towers, offered nothing in the way of escape.

Not surprisingly, Goonie's flight was quickly halted, his back plunged up against an unforgiving concrete wall, Cheekie's hot breath in his terrified face.

"You little prick!" Cheekie screamed as Harry came up beside him.

"Girl," Harry said, staring intently at Goonie.

"Huh?" Goonie asked.

Cheekie jerked Goonie forward, then slammed him back against the wall. "You heard him, you little crap, where's that frigging girlfriend of yours?"

"I . . . I..." Goonie sputtered.

"Where?" Harry asked, now a bit annoyed that his initial interrogative required further elaboration.

"She didn't show up," Goonie blurted frantically, perspiration now showing clearly beneath his arms. "I waited for her, but she didn't show up."

"Then?" Harry asked.

"Huh?"

Cheekie again slammed Goonie against the wall. "What's the matter, you don't speak frigging English? What'd you do then, ass-wipe, when the girl didn't show?"

"Nothing," Goonie whimpered, his body trembling wildly, a boy who clearly was every inch the man Javiar was not. "When she didn't show up, I just went home."

"Where?" Harry asked.

"Here," Goonie replied.

Anger spiked in Harry. He hated being misunderstood when he knew damn well he'd made himself perfectly clear. "Where?" he demanded menacingly.

Goonie looked at him blankly.

"You deaf or just stupid?" Cheekie cried. "Where's the frigging girl?"

Goonie's whole body shook. "I dunno," he pleaded. "Please. I'm telling the truth. I don't know nothing about where she is."

Harry glared at him threateningly. "Girl," he warned.

Goonie's eyes widened in animal panic. "I dunno. You can ax me a thousand times, and still I dunno."

Cheekie attempted to wrap his fingers around Goonie's neck, but they were too short and stubby for him to get a grip, so he simply returned to his earlier method of persuasion, jerked Goonie forward and slammed him back into the wall. "Where's the frigging girl?" he yelled.

Goonie's face suddenly paled, and a look of horrible embarrassment swept into his face.

"Enough," Harry said.

"Wha?" Cheekie asked.

"Home," Harry said.

Cheekie released Goonie, and he slid down on a patch of earth he himself had recently moistened.

"Pissed," Harry said as he and Cheekie headed back toward Harry's waiting car.

Goonie's humiliation clearly inspired little pity in Cheekie Putonya. "So where's the girl, you think?" he asked.

Harry shrugged silently, a gesture, as he well understood, that conveyed the full extent of what he knew.

"So what now?" Cheekie asked.

"Moon," Harry answered grimly.

Cheekie glanced skyward with a hostile glare. "Yeah, moon," he said sneeringly, as if daring that distant and celestial orb to take a piece of him.

Charlie Moon

Charlie watched the moon over Manhattan from the cramped vantage point of the small terrace of his apartment on Jones Street. It was pale and full, and it rose higher and higher in the night sky as Charlie contemplated the decline of his fortunes. Which was typical, according to Charlie, since nature, if it reacted at all to human life, generally gloated at bad luck and sneered at good luck. All you had to do was take a good look at all those pale, sickly figures who shopped in health food stores to realize just how much nature enjoyed a good laugh at human expense. There they were, buying little packets of wheat germ while big black tumors were no doubt congregating in the darkly coiled recesses of their large intestines.

Bullcrap, Charlie thought, then made a quick, angry turn and shrank back into his apartment.

Where, incidentally, he found little comfort.

The problem, of course, was Arthur Vandameer.

And the problem with Arthur was that he wanted to take back the exclusive.

And why?

Because he didn't like Charlie's politics.

Which was typical liberal illiberality, Charlie thought with a self-satisfied grunt.

But that didn't solve the problem.

Okay, so, where did wisdom lie?

Charlie contemplated the issue. Arthur Vandameer was afraid of bad press. He was afraid that Charlie would somehow make him look like an ass. Well, Arthur Vandameer WAS AN ASS, Charlie thought.

But once again, that didn't solve the problem.

Charlie tried again.

Okay, if Arthur Vandameer was afraid of being portrayed for what he was, then didn't it make perfect sense that what he really wanted was to be portrayed as what he was not?

But what was that? Charlie wondered.

No answer came, but that did not prevent Charlie from experiencing a sudden leap of piercing joy, convinced now that he ABSOLUTELY WOULD FIND a way out of the current dilemma.

As he contemplated the brilliance and wisdom of the solution he did not have, the full brilliance and wisdom of that nonexistent solution filled his heart with confidence and pride.

Yes, Charlie exulted, thinking of nothing, *yes, yes!*

He picked up the phone and dialed Arthur Vandameer's number.

"Mr. Vandameer," he said when Arthur answered, "It's Charlie Moon . . ."

"Mr. Moon," Vandermeer blurted, "I called your office but this...strange. . . ."

"We got this . . ." The voice of the new Charlie Moon suddenly emerged . . . "this mentally ill person. It's a shame, don't you think, that these people can't get the help they need?"

"Well . . . yes," Vandameer agreed.

"It's like so much these days," Charlie continued with only the faintest smile. "Whatever happened to the 'general welfare' part of the Constitution? It's as if the government simply feels no obligation to lend assistance to our less fortunate citizens."

"Uh . . . yes . . . that's true. . . ." Vandameer agreed again.

Charlie's smile broadened, and his eyes fairly glimmered in triumph. "As far as Allison is concerned," he said, now safely closing in on the details of the solution he did not have, "I think I have a solution to your problem."

"Really?" Arthur asked with what Charlie thought he heard as a sign of relief.

"Absolutely," Charlie said. "Don't worry about a thing."

"Well, what do you. . . ."

"Tomorrow," Charlie interrupted.

With that, Charlie hung up, more confident than ever that he had a solution.

The only problem, he admitted, was that he didn't.

But that was only a bump in the road, he decided, a small obstacle on the way to a bright tomorrow.

PART III

IN WHICH THE NOVEL BRIEFLY SPINS ITS WHEELS

¡QUE LIO!

Harry Stumbo

Okay, Harry thought as he sat, facing Cheekie Putonya from an all too clean, well-lighted place inside the White Castle on Fordham Road, *what now?*

Cheekie took a quick sip of coffee and set the cup down hard. "Okay," he said, "What now?"

Harry looked at the clock.

"Yeah, you're right," Cheekie said. "It's too late to do anything else." He took another sip of coffee. "We'll wait 'til tomorrow."

"Tomorrow," Harry said glumly, already contemplating the terrible changes that would no doubt mark the coming day, cleaner streets, better law enforcement, a safer city, each one a nail in the coffin of Old New York. "Change," he muttered.

Cheekie reached in his pocket and placed a varied array of curiously sticky coins on the Formica table top. "Take your pick," he said.

Roy Bumble

From the look on Bea's face, Roy discerned that the aforementioned Bea was anything but happy.

For the last few minutes, she'd bumbled about the bedroom, needlessly shifting small articles of clothing from the rowing machine to the exercise bike, both of which, along with several other pieces of impressive gym equipment had recently "fallen off a truck," but all of which, like Roy's vast collection of audio-visual equipment, Bea steadfastly refused to use because the aforementioned impressive machines had subsequently—and with only a hint of the miraculous—"fallen" fully boxed and in need of considerable assembly into Sal Pellucci's station wagon, and so, as Bea had loudly and with maximum disapproval declared, "if they were any hotter, Roy, they'd burst into flame."

That was Bea, Roy thought, honest to the core.

From his place in a bed that had, as it were, NOT fallen off a truck, Roy followed his wife's ever enlarging figure as she shifted around the Hercules and Brakeman Flex-o-Matic, ducking her head under the wide steel wingspread of the Bow-Wright Weight-Lift Center, and finally reaching the Econoline Fully Programmable Stairmaster, which, as Roy noticed, she'd conveniently converted into a six-hundred pound shoe rack.

"So," Roy said, patting the empty space to his right, "You coming to bed or what?"

"Or what," Bea chose grumpily as she drew a wrinkled pajama top from the handle of the Tension-Ease Cardiac Care Treadmill that rested upside-down beside the closet door.

For a moment, Roy considered the possibility of confronting the issue of Allison Vandameer with perfect honesty, but try as he might, he couldn't come up with any better bullcrap story than the one Allison had devised, and he had fully bought, but which Bea had—with frank contempt—utterly refused to purchase.

But what WAS she thinking, Roy wondered. Briefly he attempted to divine the meaning of Bea's obviously hostile movements, particularly the way she'd just hung a pink rubber flip-flop over the handle-bars of the mountain bike he'd only yesterday managed to prop up beside the window.

Tomorrow, he thought, now shrinking down further into the bed and easing the covers over his head, *Tomorrow, I'll* . . .

Arthur Vandameer

Arthur Vandameer sipped the last warm draught of his last cruelly expensive bottle of Dow's, and mulled over what appeared to be Charles W. Moon's sudden, perhaps even miraculous, political conversion.

As he mulled, Arthur considered the possibility that the particular Moon with whom he was now involved was not and had never been the appalling Charles W. Moon who'd written, according to the page he mulled over now, going down the list provided by Amazon.com of the works of the aforementioned Charles W., titles which, to say the least, needed no further elaboration, and which included, *The Carnivore's Guide to Mistreated Delicacies; Paddles with Holes, and Other Essays on Public Education*;

and, most egregious of all, *Let Them Eat Cant*, a mock dictionary of liberal language in which the hideous Mr. Moon had defined "reactionary" as "someone who made it" and "progressive" as "someone who didn't or did, but thinks no one else can."

Arthur sat back, stroked his chin and mulled. *Tomorrow*, he thought, *tomorrow I'll take a much closer look at Charles W. Moon.*

Allison Vandameer

Allison sat at the edge of the bed and peered about the room into which Bea Bumble had silently escorted her a few minutes before. As for Roy Bumble, he'd carefully avoided contact most of the evening as she and the aforementioned Bumbles had sat, watching Game Show Network reruns of *The Match Game*, a show whose wit and sophistication Bea Bumble seemed to find particularly amusing, especially at those rare moments when she'd actually gotten a match.

At nine, Bea had served her "specialty," which, as far as Allison had been able to make out by taste and appearance, consisted of two slices of plain white bread, each smeared with generous amounts of reduced-fat mayonnaise, then pressed together over mounds of crushed potato chips.

Allison had explained her obvious lack of appetite by saying that she was a bit under the weather. At which point she'd faked a sniffle and retired to the room she now occupied.

The problem with Bea Bumble, Allison decided, was

that she was inordinately suspicious. From the moment Roy had told the story they'd concocted at TGI Friday, Bea's small eyes had gotten smaller. She'd listened as Roy had stumbled forward, relating a fiction so simple Allison marveled that it could be doubted. And yet, doubted it had surely been.

In fact, Bea Bumble, as far as Allison could tell, had not bought a single word of it.

And so the question was, what would the aforementioned Bea do about it? Would she seek to intervene, persuade Roy to drop out of the scheme? And if so, Allison thought with a shiver of dread, what would happen to her chances of getting her Academy Award as Best Director for her groundbreaking film, *Angles*?

Tomorrow, Allison thought as a yawn came over her, her eyelids drooping sleepily, tomorrow it would all come clear.

Charlie Moon

Tomorrow would be the turning point, Charlie thought, tomorrow would decide the issue. He would wake up early, phone Arthur Vandameer and propose a breakfast meeting at THE great power breakfast location of New York, the dining room of the Regency Hotel.

Jeez, Charlie thought, imagine that, Charlie and Arthur Vandameer sitting together like old school mates, discussing politics, and—when Charlie thought the moment had arrived—the fate of Allison Vandameer, a way for Arthur to get her back, preserve his reputation, give Charlie all the credit, and then . . . ?

Charlie wasn't sure, but that didn't matter. He was sure he'd think of it tomorrow.

PART IV

DEUS EX MACHINA

WHEN THEY BEGIN THE BEGONE

Charlie Moon

More than anything, Charlie hated puns, especially those involving song titles, which he routinely dismissed as exactly the kind of semiliterate nonsense that could be expected from a generation which almost never read a book, and whose primary cultural references were about as deep as J-Lo's neckline, and no less fleeting in effect.

But still worse, Charlie thought, were the strained and sarcastic plays on the president's name that routinely dotted Arthur Vandameer's television commentaries, that Al Gore had been Bush-Whacked in Florida, for example, or the even more mindless reference to the Republican Party as the Bush League.

But all of that had to be tamped down, Charlie told himself, as he strode north on Park Avenue, the great façade of the Regency now clearly in view. No, there'd be no talk of politics on this bright and beautiful morning.

Arthur Vandameer was already seated in the far back corner of the room. Charlie made his way slowly toward him, reveling in the power he'd suddenly assumed. He glanced around the room. Nope, Jimmy Breslin was nowhere to be seen. Pete Hamill? Nah. Jerry Nachman? Uh-uh. Just Charles W. Moon!

Then, out of nowhere. . . . DISASTER!

"I've decided I don't want Allison found," Vandameer said when Charlie reached the table.

Charlie dropped like a sack of sand into the chair. "Whaaa?"

"Yes," Vandameer said. "I've given it careful thought, and I've decided that Allison must . . . find her own way."

Charlie decided to be blunt. "Her 'own way,'" he pointed out, "is with a guy named Goonie."

"Be that as it may," Vandameer replied with no visible sign of concern. "After all, it could be worse."

"Really?" Charlie tactfully inquired. "How?"

"For all Goonie's inadequacies," Vandameer answered, "He is, finally, a . . ."

"Moron?" Charlie suggested. He leaned forward and stared earnestly at Vandameer. "Okay, you can let Allison marry this guy," he said in a low, conspiratorial whisper. "But at least let me have him castrated first!"

"Dear God!" Vandameer breathed, his voice fixed in the same collusive tone. "I could never . . . I mean . . . why . . . that's absolutely horrible!"

"Oh, it's not that bad," Charlie said. "It's like when you break a guy's thumbs. After that first little pinch, they hardly scream at all."

Vandameer's eyes widened in horror. "Mr. Moon, I think that this conversation. . . ."

"Consider the consequences," Charlie said, sweet

reason now rushing him forward on a wave of sheer and certain confidence. "A long train of unhappiness. First Allison would soon be unhappy with the marriage. But by then, she'd probably have a couple of kids. They would have to suffer the pangs of an unhappy marriage, and since Allison will probably never come to you for help, because Goonie—who, please remember, IS A MORON—will never permit his wife to seek that help. These kids will be refused the kind of high-end therapeutic intervention you'd have been able to provide for them. Because of that, they will grow more and more hostile, until, in the end, they will no doubt seek some form of vengeance in—my guess is—a cruel and lawless act, the sort of high-profile outrage unhappy kids commit when they are unhappy and can't get help, and so seek to get attention by doing something dreadful, usually—dare I say always—to people otherwise wholly innocent." Charlie's eyes grew lethally intense. "You have to save those innocent people, Mr. Vandameer."

"By castrating Goonie?" Vandameer asked softly. He shook his head. "There must be another way."

Charlie leaned back and stroked his chin. "Well, yes, perhaps there is," he said. *Got him*, he thought.

But in what way?

Charlie wasn't sure, but the certainty that Arthur Vandameer was so completely GOTTEN had been so strong, along with the accompanying wave of devious delight, that Charlie had briefly let that very wave take him. Now, as the delicious water subsided, he stared blankly at Arthur Vandameer, his mind whirling through a world of "gotchas" until one of them suddenly rose to the forefront of Charlie's mind and immediately struck him as no less brilliant than the first, which seemed particularly extraordinary since the second was in direct agreement with the very proposition Vandameer had, at Charlie's arrival, immediately proposed.

"You could throw a big wedding," Charlie said.

Arthur Vandameer stared at Charlie mutely.

"A huge affair," Charlie added.

"But didn't you just say that I . . ."

"I did, yes," Charlie admitted. "But then I thought, no way would Allison go through with it and actually marry the dumb bastard."

"And that conclusion is based on what?" Arthur Vandameer inquired.

"Oh come on," Charlie said dismissively, a tactic far less perilous than his having actually to provide evidence for his latest wholly baseless conclusion. "You don't really believe that Allison would marry that guy, do you?"

"I don't know," Vandameer answered.

Charlie again rushed forward on a wave of groundless speculation. "Well, if she really wants to marry this guy, she will, right?" he said, now relying with complete confidence on his utter lack of knowledge concerning the motives, intentions, or psychological impulses of Allison Vandameer. "But if she doesn't want to marry him, and you make a big deal of throwing her a wedding, then she'll come to her senses, if you know what I mean."

To Charlie's relief, Arthur Vandameer, who, Charlie

decided, was no Einstein when it came to well . . . anything, this aforementioned none-too-bright
Vandameer actually appeared to be considering the
merits of Charlie's entirely iffy proposition.

"So I should . . . bluff?" Vandameer tentatively
inquired.

"Absolutely," Charlie said, convinced, as most child-
less people are, that only the utter lack of parental
experience can properly serve as a basis for giving
unwanted and never-heeded parental advice. A position
supported now by the fact that Arthur Vandameer still
appeared to be considering Charlie's advice despite an
intervening amount of time that should have given him
space actually to think.

Still, it was hard for Charlie to know exactly what
Vandameer was considering, since Vandameer, like
most left-wing nutcases, according to Charlie, had a
vast network of internal conflicts, all of which were
based on the simple, irreducible fact that not one of
them actually believed a single word of the aforementioned nutty ideology they publicly espoused. I mean,
Charlie thought now while Vandameer continued to
consider, I mean, would Arthur Vandameer give his
apartment back to some feather-headed Iroquois? Hell
no, Charlie said to himself with a rightward cock of his
head. Did Arthur Vandameer really spend a sleepless
hour contemplating the contribution Ted Bundy might
have made to society if the State of Florida had only
had the wisdom to let him live? No way! Did Allison go
to a public school? Uh-uh. Had Arthur Vandameer
rejected a single penny of his vast inherited wealth?

Not on your life. In fact, did any left-wing fruitcake ever reject a single social advantage despite the fact that he or she considered that advantage horribly unjust? Hell no! Not one! Charlie chuckled inwardly, remembering how, at the very end of his life, Leo Tolstoy had decided to separate himself from the corruption of owning private property by giving all he owned...TO HIS WIFE!

And so the only mystery, as far as Charlie was concerned, was how there could be so many left-wingers, when really, there WEREN'T ANY!

"Wedding," Arthur mulled, clearly going through his own particular vast network of internal conflicts. "That would prove something, wouldn't it?"

"Absolutely," Charlie said, although he couldn't guess exactly which "proof" Vandameer was considering.

"It would prove that I wasn't...prejudiced against Goonie, for either racial or class reasons."

"Yup."

"It would prove that I really believe that Allison has to make up her own mind."

"That, too."

"It would prove. . . ."

"That you're not a worthless, hypocritical ass," Charlie blurted before he could stop himself.

"Hmm, yes," Arthur said from his place in the middle of a mull. "And at the same time, it would teach Allison a lesson because, as you say, she would never marry that. . . ."

"Eskimo?"

Suddenly Vandameer's face filled with resolve. "All right, I'll do it," he said. "I'll say yes to the marriage!"

Charlie's mind raced to determine just exactly where this decision left the pube-scoop upon which his claim to fame had so firmly rested before this latest unexpected turn of events. "But . . . how," he said, buying time.

"But how what?" Arthur asked, cutting the time down considerably.

The solution came so swiftly Charlie all but gave it a Latin name. "But how will you let Allison know that you're . . . calling her bluff?"

"That's easy," Arthur said to Charlie's complete surprise. "I'll simply announce it at the end of my promo for tonight's show." Arthur suddenly glanced at his watch. "I'm taping it in fifteen minutes," he added, then rose like a rocket and hurried from the room, his bagel with a schmear hardly touched.

Charlie eyed the bagel, considered his options, then decided to pocket it, which he did on his way out, trailing Arthur Vandameer, but at a distance, since the plot had clearly thickened, and he needed to apply the clear and cleansing thinner of his mind.

He was doing just that five minutes later when his cell phone rang.

"Yes?" Charlie answered.

"Harry."

"Okay."

"Not with Goonie."

"Allison's not with Goonie?" Charlie asked. "You mean, they didn't elope?"

"Nope."

"What happened?"

"No show."

"Which one?"

"Allison."

"Okay, if she didn't meet Goonie, then where. . . ." Charlie's mind froze. "You think she might have just run away . . . or been kidnapped?"

"Maybe."

Charlie instantly returned to the night he'd walked across the square in front of the Plaza, spied none other than the now truly missing Allison Vandameer, seated with a man whose appearance he recalled vividly now, a man who might have seen something, and, best of all, a man he'd have no trouble tracking down since, he concluded with a seizure of relief, that Sherry-Netherland uniform was a dead give-away.

Harry Stumbo

Harry stopped at the corner of Broadway and 46th Street and faced Cheekie Putonya, along with the depressing wholesomeness of Times Square. "Runaway or kidnapped," he said.

"No crap," Cheekie said.

Harry shrugged.

"Well if she got snatched, who snatched her?" Cheekie, with unexpected prescience, inquired.

Harry shrugged.

"So, does that mean the job is over?"

Harry shook his head.

"So we just wait around for Moon to tell us what to do?"

Harry nodded.

"So back to Smith's Bar?" Cheekie asked.

Harry shrugged, content to return to his usual watering hole, especially since such aforementioned return was unlikely to be possible in the future given the owner's appalling determination to "spruce things up."

"Okay," Cheekie said.

Despite the early morning hour, Smith's was bustling, and to Harry's despair, this bustling did not involve an old gray mop and a metal tub foaming with industrial strength disinfectant. In the old days, the floor of Smith's would have been as sticky as the inside of a peep show booth on Christmas morning. But now, Smith's was full of tourists from the Milford Plaza, the sort who'd once only felt safe chasing the Blue Light

Special at their local Kmart, but who now felt perfectly at ease, joking and ordering egg sandwiches . . . AT SMITH'S!

"Crap," Harry said as he plopped down in the booth by the window.

Cheekie nodded. "Tourists," he sneered, clearly disappointed that none of the ones he currently eyed, and would have been more than happy to insult, was anywhere near young enough or large enough or damn mean enough to beat him to a pulp. "This Vandameer, you say he's big."

"Yeah."

"How big?"

"Huge."

"No crap," Cheekie mused. "Suppose I'll ever meet the guy?"

Harry shrugged.

"Okay, so where you think the girl is?"

Harry shrugged.

"But if Vandameer's this big, the guy who took her, he must be big too, right? Probably figures he can bully anybody, that's my guess. Just wrap his big hands around 'em and they'll cave."

"Maybe."

"Bigger than Javiar?"

"Could be."

Cheekie smiled, now clearly cooking up the series of insults he hoped to use in his relentless effort to have the crap beaten out of him. "So when we gonna meet this guy?"

Harry shrugged.

Cheekie clearly appeared disappointed that the aforementioned meeting would have to be indefinitely delayed, a disappointment that was short-lived however, since only seconds later an enormous iron worker lumbered into the bar, elbowing his way among the Blue Light Specials until he reached the table next to Cheekie's.

"Don't," Harry said in appropriate sotto voce.

Cheekie sniffed the air. "I smell Alpo," he said loudly, then whirled around to face the iron worker. "Hey, lard-ass, if you're gonna sit next to me, don't kiss your wife next time."

THYME AND TIED

Roy Bumble

Roy sat in front of the television, Allison still asleep in the adjoining room, but Bea wide awake in the more closely adjoining beige recliner, clearly wondering why, out of nowhere, he, the aforementioned Roy, had suddenly taken an interest in *Speaking Truth to Power with Arthur Vandameer.*

"I think I should be more informed," Roy explained, his eyes fixed on the set because he knew that if they even once slid over toward Bea, she'd see he was lying his head off.

"Informed about what?" Bea shrewdly inquired.

"You know," Roy explained. "Politics."

Bea's small eyes contracted.

"Current events is what I'm saying," Roy added, his gaze now locked on the flickering screen.

On the television, Arthur Vandameer was talking about the various topics he intended to address on his eight o'clock show, not one of which had a thing to do either with Allison Vandameer, or the six-figure sum Roy had, at least in his mind, already collected and spent on a great apartment in Manhattan. There was stuff about war and peace, privatizing Social Security, how "President Big Brother" was chewing away at Joe Public's "freedom of choice," a freedom to which Roy had trouble relating since, when he stopped to think about it, his own exercise of choice had always been pretty much used up in deciding between Big Mac or Kentucky Fried.

Then, just as Allison staggered blearily out of the bedroom and stood, blinking sleepily at the screen, Vandameer leaned forward, peered earnestly into the camera and said, "Now, on a personal note, I'd like to offer my daughter, Allison and her fiancé, Joselito Castillo de la Mancha Diaz, my best wishes for a very happy marriage. Good luck, kids."

Roy's gaze shot over to Allison, who stared thunder-struck at the screen, as Arthur Vandameer smiled sweetly then dissolved to black, both of them, as Roy suddenly realized, intently observed by Bea Bumble, whose eyes worked on them like red-hot needles.

Under that searing gaze, Roy said to Allison, "So, you'd better get over to the . . ."

"Shoot," Allison said, then made a lightning turn, rushed back into the bedroom, and emerged again, sec-onds later, her early astonishment at Art's unexpected public announcement of the Allison-Goonie nuptials now entirely dissolved.

"It's a bluff," she said confidently as she and Roy stepped out of the apartment.

"You sure?" Roy asked.

"He doesn't believe I'll go through with it."

"But you're not . . . are you?"

Allison looked at Roy as if he had two heads. "Of course not. Unless my father drives me to it. Which I can't let him do. Which means I have to do something first."

Roy stared at her, confused but unwilling to state the exact nature of his confusion, nor the fact that the previously spent six-figure income had just been sucked back into the realm of the highly improbable, the great Manhattan apartment now relegated to the bleak ground in which both the Russian silver mine and the gently loping Speed Trap had previously been buried.

Briefly, the two waited in silence until the elevator arrived, at which arrival they stepped inside and descended to the street.

Once outside, Allison glanced about the luxurious reaches of Queens Boulevard, then turned to Roy. "We have to bluff his bluff."

"We do?" Roy inquired. "How?"

Allison's eyes rolled skyward. "Wedding invitations." Her smile struck Roy as very nearly reptilian. "That should do the trick."

"Wedding invitations?" Roy asked.

Allison seemed not to hear the quizzical nature of his response. "Which way to Tiffany?" she asked.

Charlie Moon

Charlie closed in on the entrance to the Sherry-Netherland like a man on a mission. He knew that the pube-scoop now rested in a somewhat precarious position. He'd somewhat impulsively provided Arthur

Vandameer with a route out of his dilemma, and to Charlie's now admitted surprise, Vandameer had no less impulsively accepted it. But what Vandameer didn't know, Charlie reasoned as he stood, peering toward the hotel's elegant glass doors, was that Allison's elopement had been forestalled by a . . . what?

Charlie didn't know.

Kidnapping?

If this were the case, then it followed that a ransom demand would presently arrive at the auspicious digs of Arthur Vandameer, and if that happened . . . why . . . it would be. . . .

Perfect! Charlie decided as he continued to run the pube-scoop scenario, himself now effortlessly placed at the center of the drama.

But where exactly might that drama go?

Charlie considered the increasingly attractive possibilities.

What if the kidnapping were followed by foul play? Allison buried alive somewhere on Long Island, say?

Not bad, Charlie reasoned, except of course for Allison.

Even better was a scenario that had Allison rescued from the evil clutches of her kidnappers?

Oh yes, Charlie thought, much better!

And better still would be Allison rescued from the evil clutches of her kidnappers by . . . CHARLIE MOON!

Fan-Frigging-Tastic!

Charlie smiled in that idyllic and joyous way he

always smiled when reality took a hike and he was able to drift for a moment on the warm, soothing currents of pure delusion.

Then a cold breeze struck, bringing an unfortunate fact into collision with his small, frail craft.

Problem 1) He didn't know if Allison had been kidnapped.

Problem 2) If she had been, he didn't know who'd done it.

But that's why he'd come to the Sherry-Netherland, after all, Charlie thought, now beating back the harsh and very-alarming winds of reality. He smiled at his new role: *Charlie Moon, Crime-Buster.*

Arthur Vandameer

Arthur Vandameer felt absolutely splendid!

Why?

Because, he'd actually acted according to his own, unassailable moral principles. . . . AND NOT SUFFERED HORRIBLE CONSEQUENCES FOR DOING SO!

The same could not be said of his earlier determinations to stand by certain similarly unassailable moral principles.

For example, it could not be said of his decision to rid himself of stock in South African companies.

Nor could it be said of his decision to avoid investments in any bank that pressed its heavy debt load upon impoverished third world countries.

It couldn't even be said of his decision to become a

vegetarian, or his steadfast refusal to buy Diana a fur coat for their first anniversary.

In fact, the economic, emotional and, in the case of the fur, even romantic consequences of these earlier staunch adherences to his unassailable moral principles, had been so severe that Arthur had failed staunchly to adhere to a single one of them. And thus, had guiltily watched the value of his portfolio skyrocket even as Diana pranced down Fifth Avenue in her new sealskin coat, the two of them headed for their anniversary dinner at Keene's Steakhouse.

But this time it was different, Arthur exulted as he made his way out of the studio and into the midmorning bustle of Sixth Avenue, the glittering offices of World News International Network just behind him, its lighted zipper relating the details of a vast and staggeringly lethal tidal wave that had struck a remote Polynesian island, a hideously tragic event that, as Arthur failed to notice, did absolutely nothing to deflate the current buoyancy of his mood.

"That was a curious announcement," Roland Fitzwater, founder, CEO and majority stockholder in WNIN, the man to whom Arthur answered, and who had steadfastly supported his ever more leftward tilt despite the warnings of lesser network executives whose complaints he, the aforementioned Roland Fitzwater, had fended off with the terse comment, "What's the matter, you can't take a joke?"

"It was a matter of principle," Arthur (the aforementioned joke) Vandameer replied proudly.

"What principle was involved in wishing your

daughter a happy marriage?" Fitzwater asked, clearly unable to understand exactly what Arthur had put on the line at the end of his morning promo.

"Well," Arthur explained, "after all . . ."

Fitzwater peered at Vandameer quizzically.

"After all, the groom is. . . ."

"Is what, Arthur?"

"The groom is. . . ." Arthur chose his words carefully, and in so doing, left out all reference to ethnicity or class. ". . . not very knowledgeable about history."

Fitzwater laughed. "That's nothing, Arthur. My son-in-law thinks that Lincoln invented the Town Car." He pointedly tapped the rim of the enormous white cowboy hat that was his signature. "Now tell me the truth, Arthur, what's this 'matter of principle' you're talking about?"

Arthur swallowed hard, a sign of distress that Roland Fitzwater clearly did not fail to miss.

"Let me guess," Fitzwater said with a cunning grin. "I'll just wager there's something wrong with Allison's intended." He laughed. "What is he, blind? Crippled? Does he perhaps suffer from explosive bowel syndrome?"

Arthur knew that Roland's mention of the latter affliction was based upon a condition from which Arthur himself suffered, and which he now realized he would have been well-served to keep secret, rather than weepily revealing its often embarrassing consequences to Madelyn Boyd on a night during which Arthur had drunk too much to keep his bowel problems to himself and Madelyn had drunk too little not to remember every word of a drunken confession she had clearly passed on to none other than Roland Fitzwater, Arthur's boss, but also, as was now distressingly apparent, his rival in bed.

"No, he's. . . ." Arthur stopped, unable to say exactly what Goonie was.

Fitzwater's face froze, but behind the fixed stare, Arthur could see that the mind of his former benefactor and protector at WNIN was violently astir. "You really don't approve of this lad, do you?"

"No," Arthur admitted, "I don't."

"And why not, may I ask?"

"Well," Arthur stalled. "It's just that . . . well . . ."

"You consider him totally unfit as a son-in-law, am I right?" Fitzwater asked, an odd gleam in his eye.

"Totally."

"This is a very common phenomenon, Arthur," Fitzwater said. "You shouldn't be upset about it. As I say, it's very, very common. You might even say, widespread. Which means that it's something a large segment of the viewing audience has no doubt felt at one time or another."

"You think so?" Arthur asked hesitantly, unaware of where this line of discussion might be going, but convinced that it was going somewhere, and that this somewhere was probably a place he wasn't going to like.

"Absolutely," Fitzwater answered. "Which is why you should bring him on your show."

"What!" Arthur cried. "Bring . . . Goonie?"

"Goonie!" Fitzwater yelped. His face seemed suddenly bathed in beatific light. "Is that the fellow's name?"

"More of a . . . nickname?" Arthur admitted weakly.

"And the nickname is . . . fitting?" Fitzwater asked pointedly.

"Uh . . . well."

"So this young man is a bit lacking in intellectual prowess?" Fitzwater asked with unimpaired delight.

"He's well . . ." Arthur said.

"Goonie!" Fitzwater cried, this time adding a fierce clap of the hands as an added show of enthusiasm. "That's rich, Arthur. That's really rich. Definitely wonderful material for a great show. You MUST have him on. An interview, just think of it, an interview. Prospective father-in-law and son-in-law. What an opportunity!"

Arthur stared at Fitzwater, thunderstruck at the idea of actually talking to Goonie Castillo de la Mancha Diaz on national television. "But," he stammered . . . "But . . . but."

"Think of it, Arthur," Fitzwater steamed on like a great belching train. "Think of the point you could make. All these years you've represented a cardinal value, the fact that a person shouldn't be judged by his race or religion or class, or even how frigging dumb he is!"

"Yes . . . but . . ."

"A complete damn idiot has the same humanity as anyone else, isn't that what you've said, Arthur?'"

"Well . . ."

"Damn right!" Fitzwater shouted, now lifting his fist into the air. "'True humanitarianism rests on blindness to fault,'" he quoted. "Isn't that what you said when you defended the right of that wild-haired freak to use that small-town library in tiny Otisville, Nebraska? You remember that freak don't you, Arthur, the one who stank the place up, and scared the old people, and yelled at the kids, and pissed in the card catalogue."

"Well, that was. . . ."

"But regardless of all that, he had a right to use the library, wasn't that your position, Arthur?"

'Well . . . yes . . . but."

"And what did you base that position on?" Roland asked, his hand now even higher in the air. "That this offensive bag of stink was a HUMAN BEING!"

"Yes, and . . ."

"'True humanitarianism rests on blindness to fault,'" Fitzwater repeated, his voice now full and orotund, as if Arthur's moral position had actually been his own, which Arthur knew it wasn't, since Fitzwater, himself, had led a savage fight to keep a proposed SRO from spewing its tidal wave of unfortunate humanity into the otherwise pristine atmosphere of East 73rd Street. "That was a great show, Arthur. And remember the mail it generated? Why people thought you . . . I mean . . . people were . . . really. . . ." He stopped. "It got a huge response, that program."

"Eighty-seven death threats," Arthur said, "Horse feces in a shoe box. Several envelopes filled with mysterious substances." Arthur's features paled. "Not to mention that body part."

"It was a fake," Fitzwater said with a dismissive chuckle. "Not a real . . . member. And besides, what did the nature of that response show, Arthur, except that you'd struck a nerve in the general public? That's what a commentator is supposed to do, isn't he? Strike a nerve? Get a response."

"Eyeballs in a jar of formaldehyde?" Arthur asked.

"I still use it as a paperweight," Fitzwater laughed. "Surely you didn't consider it a cause for alarm."

Arthur started to answer, but Fitzwater rushed on.

"Think of it, Arthur," he said. "A full hour. You and this . . . educationally deprived youngster."

"He thinks Iran is in Canada," Arthur blurted.

"Also geographically deprived," Fitzwater continued. "And which of our splendid public schools does he attend?"

"I don't know . . . but."

"It doesn't matter anyway," Fitzwater said. "But imagine it, Arthur, you and this lad, sitting face-to-face, discussing history, politics . . . LIFE! The boy clearly lacks certain fundamental information, but that doesn't matter, because he is, first of all, a human being, and because of that you must be fully accepting of him. Not only as a fellow human being . . . BUT AS A SON-IN-LAW! The guy who's gonna plug your only daughter, get her big with child . . . the whole enchilada. This is the guy you must welcome him into your family without hesitation. Because, Arthur . . ."True humanitarianism rests . . .'"

"Yes, yes," Arthur interrupted.

"I tell you it's perfect," Fitzwater gushed. "Especially given the fact that I'd already decided to pump up the volume on your show."

"Pump up the volume?"

"A title change for example."

"What's the matter with *Speaking Truth to Power*?"

Fitzwater gazed at Arthur like a father explaining the facts of life to a retarded son. "Well, it's a little . . . flat."

Arthur hesitated a moment, then asked the dread question. "And what was the new title you had in mind?"

Fitzwater beamed. "*Left of Mental*," he said proudly.

"*Left of Mental?*"

"Exactly," Fitzwater answered. "Rolls off the tongue, don't you think?"

"But what does it . . . mean?"

"That the show's a little, well, kookie."

"Kookie?"

"So we can pull in the idiot fringe audience," Fitzwater explained. "Especially the young idiot fringe. The type that otherwise would be watching Beavis and Butt-head."

"Beavis and Butt-head!" Arthur blurted.

"Or maybe Jerry Springer."

"Jerry Springer!" Arthur yelped.

"Right," Fitzwater said. "Which is why this idea of you having a heart to heart with this . . . Goonie . . . is a great idea." He laughed. "Just think of it as the political equivalent of say, *Grudge Match*." His smile broadened with delight. "Think of it, Arthur, you'll be on the cutting edge. A show not just of commentary, but of mindless confrontation." An idea appeared to spark. "And, you know, a touch of, well, physicalness—or is it physicality? Anyway, it wouldn't hurt."

Arthur's lips parted wordlessly.

"Physicalness," Fitzwater decided. "A touch of physicalness wouldn't hurt the show."

"Physical . . . ness?"

"Violence," Fitzwater said cheerily. He leaned over slightly. "So, if you could arrange for this Goonie fellow to take a swing at you on the air, well, all the better, know what I mean?"

"Take a swing?"

"Don't worry," Fitzwater said. "You'll have pepper spray if he gets out of hand."

"But Roland," Arthur said weakly, "This all sounds a bit . . . well . . . frivolous."

Fitzwater's eyes were cold blue arctic lakes. "Well, facts are facts, Arthur. And certainly you wouldn't want to see the show . . . decline."

Decline. The dreaded word.

Arthur felt a blade of terror rake his spine. "Are the ratings . . . declining?"

Fitzwater gave Arthur a darkly significant look, paused a moment so that its import could be properly absorbed, then clapped his hands together. "So, make whatever arrangements you need to get you and your daughter's boyfriend before the cameras."

Goonie? Arthur thought. Before the cameras? With me?

The very thought of such a confrontation filled Arthur with horror. "But . . ." he stammered, "But . . . when?"

"We'll tape it tonight," Fitzwater declared.

"Tonight?" Arthur stammered. "But I don't even know where Goonie is."

"Oh, don't worry," Fitzwater said confidently. "I'll find him."

"But . . . Roland . . . I don't think that. . . ."

Roland Fitzwater stared down at him from the great tower of his financial backing. "Decline, Arthur," he warned. "Decline."

ME GUSTAN LOS CACAUATES

Bea Bumble

Bea Bumble kept her distance, though she wasn't sure she needed to, since Roy would never have suspected her following behind him, particularly disguised in the peanut costume she'd yanked from the closet just after Roy and that little slut who was trying to get him involved in some kind of shady deal had hurriedly left the apartment. Bea had acquired the costume during her short stint in the "marketing department" of Mr. Salty Peanuts, her duties pretty much confined to palming off small packs of salted peanuts to the crowds that swirled around Macy's from Thanksgiving to New Year's. True, it was not a costume that allowed for much ventilation, and even now she could feel the temperature building inside its woolen skin, but if getting overheated was the price she had to pay for keeping Roy on the straight and narrow, then overheated she would get.

Besides, as a disguise the peanut suit was perfect. A perfection that had, in fact, already been demonstrated on those very recent occasions when Roy had glanced back at the trailing Mr. Salty as he and the little slut made their way toward the subway station off Queens

Boulevard, then again as Mr. Salty had taken a seat just opposite him, and yet a third time as Mr. Salty had continued to trail Roy and the aforementioned little slut up Fifth Avenue, where, Bea feared, the little slut would continue to lure him into the iron grip of dishonesty.

The exact nature of this move was not exactly clear, but Bea was pretty sure it would involve the little slut's long white fingers going somewhere they didn't belong, and at that moment, according to her plan, Mr. Salty in pure peanut rage would strike, the little slut would be severely disciplined, and Roy would be rescued from the clutches of a youthful seductress who, Bea had to admit, she could hardly blame for being enthralled.

For Roy Bumble was, after all, quite a hunk of male-meat, and because of that Bea had always suspected that the day would come when some little slut would make the very attempt this particular little slut was clearly making. In the same sense, she'd always known the course she would take in response to the little hussy's shameless attempt to steal her, Bea's, Roy. She would take up the rod—in this case, Mr. Salty's long wooden cane—and flail the living hell out of the offending female party. Then she would take Roy home and explain to him that a guy with his kind of sex appeal had to be careful, especially with impressionable little sluts who were trying to involve him in some sort of illicit enterprise.

She had no doubt that Roy would understand what she meant, even though, as far as she'd ever been able to tell, Roy remained utterly unaware of the animal passion he evoked in other women. That was part of his charm, Bea decided, as once again Roy stopped, glanced back, peered closely at Mr. Salty, then turned slowly and headed forward again, the little slut looking cranky and waving him forward as if she were already the boss, Roy her co-conspirator, and Bea just another heartbroken female he had left behind.

Charlie Moon

Fydor Polanovich was an Eastern European stereotype Charlie had seen before, a hard-working guy whose green card had probably been red as an orangutan's ass before he'd gotten sick of movies about tractors, slunk off to the West, and finally made it to a country where workers weren't expected to like opera.

Thus having reduced Fydor Polanovich to a pre-post-communist-capitalist caricature, Charlie said, "My name's Charlie Moon. You got a guy works here, wears a long gray coat with gold epaulettes. Doorman, maybe, or elevator guy. Chunky. About fifty. You got a guy like that, right?"

Polanovich eyed Charlie suspiciously. "You friend heem?"

Polanovich didn't seemed to realize that he'd actually answered the question, but that was typical, Charlie thought, of guys like Polanovich, former communist-blockheads, more brawn than brain, guys who took hours with the *TV Guide* crossword, and usually gave up on clues like, *Three letter rodent.*

"He could be a witness," Charlie added.

"What he see?" Polanovich asked.

"A girl in the park."

"Lot girl in park," Polanovich opined.

"Look, Igor, can we cut to the chase here," Charlie said impatiently. "I'm a reporter for the *Register*. I'm looking for a girl who happens to be rich and who happens to be missing, and whom I, myself, saw sitting near the Plaza with a guy in a Sherry-Netherland uniform not more than fifteen minutes before she vanished." Since he still had room on the one long breath he'd sucked in before beginning, Charlie continued. "So the thing is, this highly unskilled laborer may or may not be the subject of my investigation, that is, he may or may not have done bodily harm to the rich girl who . . . as I say . . . IS FRIGGING MISSING!" He stopped, drew in a short one. "Now, who is this guy and where is this guy, and did you see this guy last night?"

Charlie realized that he'd asked at least two too many questions when Polanovich answered, "No."

Charlie guessed that Polanovich had, in fact, responded only to the last of his multiple interrogatives. "Why not? When I saw him, he was wearing his uniform."

This fact, whose import for the aforementioned unskilled laborer's potential for further employment at the Sherry-Netherland seemed only now to have occurred to Fydor Polanovich, suddenly appeared to sink like a black stain into his, the aforementioned Fydor's, none-too-porous mind. "He call in seek."

"Seek? I mean . . . sick?"

"That what he say when he call."

"So you didn't see him?"

"No."

This negative returned Charlie to the first of his previous questions. "What's this guy's name?"

"Roy," Polanovich answered. "Roy Bumble."

An answer whose thoroughness allowed Charlie to proceed to the penultimate question of his previously tripartite query.

"Where's this Roy Bumble live?"

"Queens. 12 82nd Road."

Charlie nodded. "He expected in tonight?"

"Yes," Polanovich said. "Four this afternoon."

Charlie smiled. "Thanks, Olaf."

"Fydor," Polanovich corrected sternly. "My name Fydor."

Charlie leaned forward and brought his lips very near to Polanovich's curiously gnarled right ear. "A word of advice," he whispered, "Change it to Freddy."

Polanovich grimaced. "Anything you say, Harley," he sneered.

Charlie knew when he was getting it back in his face, but deepening the confrontation with a pint-sized, probably still pro-Commie cigarette butt like Freddy Polanovich hardly seemed worthwhile. And so, rather than grabbing for Freddy's collar, he reached for his cell phone and dialed the number.

"Harry? Charlie. Where are you?"

"Smith's."

"I'll be there in fifteen minutes."

"Stay."

"Right."

"Cheekie?"

"Tell him to hang around too," Charlie said. "I got another job for the both of you."

Roy Bumble

Roy glanced back just as Mr. Salty ducked behind a convenient corner.

"Did you see that?" he asked urgently.

Allison seemed not to hear him, her eyes already fiendishly agleam as she peered at a diamond tiara in Tiffany's window. "Okay," she said, "Let's go." Then she briskly waved Roy forward and pranced into the store.

Roy had never set foot inside Tiffany & Co., but it was clear that its floors and terraces were as familiar to Allison as the Slim-Fast aisle at Pathmark was to Bea.

Once past the front door, Allison hastily bounded eastward, her long blond hair flipping right and left until she reached the luxuriously paneled elevators at the back of the building. At that point, she punched the Up, then stepped inside the elevator, punched 3, and together she and Roy silently drifted heavenward until the elevator doors opened again, this time onto a large, elegantly appointed room lined with desks behind which sat a primly dressed army of "specialists."

Allison's specialist was a woman who wore a small brass nameplate upon which the name Gloria Pendergast had been inscribed.

"Good morning, Allison," Ms. Pendergast said as Allison, bounding once again, approached the afore-mentioned specialist's beautiful mahogany desk.

"I'm getting married," Allison announced. "It's going to be quite a large affair. For a start, I'd like to select my invitations."

"And how many invitations will you need?" Ms. Pendergast asked, her eyes only occasionally moving toward Roy, whom she seemed to consider Allison's burly and none too sapient bodyguard.

Allison's eyes rolled upward, as if only the infinitude of space could hold the number she then conjured. "Fifteen thousand," she said lightly.

Roy sucked in an astonished breath.

"Embossed in gold," Allison added.

"Of course," Ms. Pendergast replied.

"And with matching return envelopes and RSVP."

"Of course."

Again Allison's heavenly blue eyes drifted . . . well . . . heavenward. "And I'd like some little identifying mark."

"Of course."

Allison probed her right dimple with an inquisitive finger. "How about a peacock feather in each invitation."

To Roy's amazement, this added detail did not appear unusual to Ms. Pendergast. "Tail or wing?" she asked.

"Let me see, a tail feather would be quite large, wouldn't it?"

"It would," Ms. Pendergast agreed. "And, of course, rather impressive."

Allison smiled. "Tail it is, then," she said, then thought better of it, and added: "No, no. A tail with the invitation, and a wing for the RSVP."

Ms. Pendergast nodded. "And the invitation will be for the wedding, itself?" she asked.

"Oh no," Allison cried, as if half-offended by the suggestion.

"Of course," Ms. Pendergast said.

"This is only for the engagement party," Allison added.

"Of course."

"For the wedding, I'll want something REALLY GRAND."

"Of course."

Allison reached for her purse and whipped out a platinum American Express card. "My fiance's name is Goonie," she said cheerily.

Ms. Pendergast's smile betrayed nothing. "Of course," she said as she snatched, with considerable agility, the aforementioned platinum from Allison's delicate pink hand.

Arthur Vandameer

Arthur Vandameer was in deep doo-doo, and he knew it.

Left of Mental?

A show meant to attract the idiot fringe?

Beavis and Butt-head?

From his place at the China Grill, Arthur watched the assorted media movers and shakers as they power-lunched. In their esteemed presence, as he suddenly and distressingly realized, he felt . . . well . . . small.

Before his meeting with Roland Fitzwater, he'd been Arthur Vandameer, commentator-at-large, liberal gad-fly, a left-wing H.L. Mencken, espouser of appallingly unpopular views, convinced, as the title of his show had so clearly suggested, that truth would win out.

But clearly something else had outed, and Arthur knew all too well what that something else was. He heard it in the sly way Roland Fitzwater had threatened him, *You certainly wouldn't want to see the show . . . decline.*

Decline!

The word struck again with the same cold horror.

Decline. His ratings were in decline!

Arthur again had the sensation of shrinking, only this time the sensation was so strong he wondered that his clothes didn't swallow him, that, to the Paul Bunyan-sized movers and shakers gathered beneath the high ceiling of the China Grill, he didn't look like a lit-tle boy in his father's suit.

Decline!

Arthur swallowed hard, motioned for the waiter, and ordered another scotch. When it came, he took a long pull, set down the glass, and sternly considered the actions he might take along with Fitzwater's response.

Action One: He could refuse to change the show.

Fitzwater's response: Cancel the show.

Action Two: He could make a counter-suggestion as to how to improve the show. He could have more showbiz people as guests, for example. Particularly showbiz people who were drug addicts or thieves or murderers, or just suffering from some dreadful, degenerative disease. He could combine these appearances with political discussion.

One such discussion immediately came to mind:

Arthur: So, O.J. where do you stand on making the tax cut permanent?

O.J.: Well, as you know, Arthur, my personal retirement accounts . . .

With an audible gasp of horror, Arthur abruptly brought the imagined interview to a close, though not before conjuring Fitzwater's response: *Do you think you could get O.J. to take a swing at you?*

Action Three: He could give it a try. He could . . . interview Goonie?

No! Arthur determined with an absolute determination to maintain his show's integrity that melted instantaneously, like ice cream in a microwave.

But why, Arthur wondered, had his adamantine determination to maintain the integrity of his show so quickly liquefied?

Certainly it wasn't a question of his needing the income it provided. He had no need of income since he'd long ago inherited his mother's money . . . which

was actually his father's money, or at least that part of
the old man's fortune that the old duffer hadn't squan-
dered on Rolex watches and amorous escapades before
his wife, the aforementioned mother, had for the most
part legally wrested control of the estate, sold the
watches, closed the bank accounts, evicted from entirely
separate luxury apartments an exceedingly blonde
woman named Flo and a redhead named Bubbles, liq-
uidated a series of poorly performing mutual funds,
then sensibly invested this shrewdly and, for the most
part, lawfully acquired capital in solid American banks
to whom a host of impoverished Latin American countries were fiendishly in debt.

Okay, Arthur said to himself. So why can't I just tell
Fitzwater to stuff it, and walk away from the show?

The answer, when it came, was as devastating as it
was obvious.

The envelope, please . . . And the answer is?

Without the show, Arthur Vandameer would be forgotten faster than a favor.

Without the show, Arthur Vandameer would be . . .
just Arthur Vandameer.

Taken together, these two truths outed a third and
yet more penetrating glimpse into the obvious:

Without the show, Arthur Vandameer . . . WOULD
BE NOTHING!

In a frenzy of self-loathing, Arthur brought his
entire life under ruthless scrutiny, an exercise which,
for all its devastating thoroughness, lasted no more
than three seconds, after which, with all his many defi-
ciencies minutely analyzed, Arthur was now free to fol-

low his favorite impulse beyond that of social improvement, and which was, as might be expected, merely the
micro of that wholly worthy macro, that is to say . . . the
improvement of himself.

Which was a work, he realized instantly, that could
only be carried out in an atmosphere of quiet reflection, an atmosphere that could not be satisfactorily
maintained unless his inner world was calm, which
meant that he had to do whatever was necessary to calm
the inward storm, which meant that above all—and no
matter how he had to change it—Arthur Vandameer
HAD TO KEEP HIS SHOW!

In this effort, Arthur thought as he brought the
scotch once again to his lips, he had one advantage, the
famously short attention span of Roland Matheson
Fitzwater.

The shallowness of Fitzwater's concentration had
first come to light when, out of nowhere, he'd suggested a radio program called *Painting for Radio* in which
learned scholars would actually describe paintings to
what Fitzwater believed would doubtless be a vast and
continually enthralled radio audience. This idea had
been dropped not because wiser heads had prevailed,
but because the idea had simply and summarily
dropped from Fitzwater's brain.

Still later, at a legendary repast on Fitzwater's
Connecticut estate, the founder, CEO and majority
stockholder of WNIN had proposed a weekly movie
series called *Stories This Time*. The idea was to buy a
large stock of foreign movies, mostly French, then
recut them so that they actually had plots. *Claire's Knee*,

for example, was to be reissued as *Claire's Fee*, the "story this time" revolving around a teenaged prostitute's seaside escapades.

Fitzwater's passionate presentation of *Stories This Time* had lasted nearly fifteen minutes, after which, quite literally, it had vanished.

Over the years, similarly absurd notions had so often risen to Fitzwater's brain, effervesced briefly, then wholly evaporated, that certain disgruntled executives had dubbed him "Fizz-Water."

Fitzwater's incapacity to hold an idea longer than a red-hot rivet now struck Arthur as his only salvation. If he could simply stall for time, Goonie would disappear, and with Goonie, the whole notion of radically changing *Speaking Truth To Power*.

Briefly Arthur considered how he might remove Goonie from Fitzwater's mind. One thing was sure, he decided, the marriage had to be stopped since as long as Goonie had the potential, either realizable or not, of being part of the Vandameer family, he would be part of the Fitzwater consciousness. And so the marriage, and even any further discussion of such nuptials, had to be brought immediately to an end.

And so Allison had to be found right away and returned to her senses.

And Goonie?

No doubt about it, Arthur concluded, Goonie had to disappear.

NO TICKEE- NO WASHEE

Goonie

Goonie stared at the large, full-color map of the United States and wondered what the point of knowing where some place was if you weren't going there.

Kansas?

Jeez, he was never going to Kansas. Who would go to places that began with a K?

"The Midwest is known as the breadbasket of the United States," Mr. Corcoran declared, his little pointed stick now sweeping over the center of the map, which just looked like the rest of the map, as far as Goonie could see, and in that sense, didn't look at all like a slice of bread.

But that wasn't the big question, as far as Goonie's curiosity about geography was concerned. What he really wanted to know was how deep you had to go to swim under an island. But when he'd finally worked up the courage to ask Mr. Corcoran that very question, the old fart had just stared at him silently for a moment then said, with a shrug, "You couldn't hold your breath that long, Joselito."

WELL DUH! Goonie thought. Crap, he already knew that!

And so now he sat back, folded his arms over his chest, and did what he usually did at times when he had to sit down. He thought of Allison.

These thoughts were anything but clear.

For example, he began, where the hell is she?

Here he was, sitting right where she and Javiar had agreed he should sit, facing General Sh, sitting there until his ass bones had practically poked through his jeans, sitting there knowing that if Javiar came by, which, of course, he damn did, he'd get his ears pulled all the way back to Co-op City.

And then, on top of that, two guys show up and Javiar, with his usual lack of patience, bounces one of the guys from wall to wall until the guy is, well, not dead, damn it,

because if Javiar had finished the job, that embarrassing lawn sprinkling episode would never have happened, and his mother would not have had to inquire, "*Que lio, Joselito. Que pasa? Los pantalones, tan mojada . . .*" and so on until Goonie had finally come up with the only explanation he was sure his mother would believe, namely that he'd forgotten to take off his pants before climbing into the shower . . . AGAIN!

Which, following the zigzag circuitry of his thought, returned Goonie to the original conundrum: WHERE THE HELL IS SHE?!

Another guy.

This was a stinging possibility, and each time Goonie considered it, his mind swirled with appalling visions of Allison swooning giddily in this other guy's arms. The action was always fevered, and he was always outside a thick window, peering in, but not silently. Oh no. He was screaming at the top of his voice. ALLISON! ALLISON!

But she kept right on doing what she was doing, which really wasn't that bad, he sometimes thought, since even President Hillary's husband had said it wasn't really sex.

But then again, it sure looked like sex, and he damn sure bet Father Feliz would say it was sex, and so he had to conclude that although maybe it wasn't sex . . . IT SURE DID LOOK LIKE IT.

So the question now was, WHERE THE HELL IS SHE?

The circle once again completed, Goonie, now incontestably suffering from the numbing effects of too much thinking, closed his eyes and settled in for a long merciful release from the rigors of trying to figure out in precisely what way the Midwest looked like bread.

He was not sure how long this pleasant retreat from information lasted before he was rudely awakened by a poke from Mr. Corcoran's stick.

"Someone wants to see you, Joselito," Mr. Corcoran told him.

"Me?" Goonie inquired with a complementary jerk of his own thumb toward none other than his own person.

"He's in the hall," Mr. Corcoran said.

Goonie assumed the "someone" who awaited him in the hallway was in some way connected to law enforcement, but the large smile that greeted him as the man came forward, hand outstretched, suggested to Goonie that the aforementioned someone was not, in fact, looking for Goonie at all, but instead for some other kid who, unlike Goonie, knew who the someone was.

"Goonie!" the man cried. "Great to meet you, son."

Son? Goonie asked himself. Could it be that Javiar was not his father?

"Roland Fitzwater here," the man said as he grabbed Goonie's hand and pumped it vigorously. "Congratulations are in order, I understand."

Goonie could not imagine for what he was being congratulated unless by some completely unfathomable means this Mr. Fitzwater had learned that Goonie could stand on one leg longer than anyone else at the High School of Mechanical Arts, a feat he had not demonstrated since sixth grade but which he now assumed to be far more renowned than he'd previous realized.

"So, you're the lucky fellow who's engaged to Allison Vandameer," the man said, still pumping Goonie's decidedly fish-limp hand.

"You know where she is?" Goonie asked, a wave of excitement now sweeping over him at the prospect of having the thorny issue of "where the hell is she" momentarily resolved.

"Not at the moment," the man answered. He tapped the wide brim of his enormous cowboy hat. "But more important, I know where you are."

WELL DUH, Goonie thought. Crap, even I know that!

"But even more important than your current whereabouts, my boy," the man continued, "I know where you're going to be at eight o'clock this evening." The man's smile broadened. "And just where do you think that might be, son?"

Goonie did the calculations. Okay, Thursday + seven o'clock = Rice and beans with Javiar. "Having rice and beans with Javiar?" he answered with an unexpected confidence that he might actually be right.

"Huh?" the man asked. Then he laughed. "Oh no, my boy! You are going to be the featured guest on the *Arthur Vandameer Show*."

Goonie had never seen the *Arthur Vandameer Show*, but he immediately assumed that it involved some kind of game, that he might well have to dress in a weird costume, and, worst of all, that as "featured guest" he would probably have to eat something disgusting like the people on *Fear Factor*.

On that thought the question "where the hell is she," which had wholly occupied Goonie's mind for the last eighteen hours was swept away, replaced by a far deeper and more immediate concern: *Could it be bull balls?*

Bea Bumble

The one thing Bea hadn't guessed as she trailed Roy and the little slut north on Fifth Avenue, was just how hot a peanut costume could get. It was like being in a plastic bubble, her own ample flesh generating warmth like an electric space heater. A situation made no better by the fact that the little slut seemed to be steadily quickening her pace, leading poor Roy from one shop to the next, though always emerging without even a small brown bag to show for it. Perhaps, Bea thought, perhaps that was part of the little slut's plan. She probably knew that Roy's investments had not panned out, and so she was showing him that she could shop and shop, and just enjoy the shopping, never buying anything, so that Roy would finally get the message that she only wanted to be with him, and at that point, the little slut would . . . do something with her hands.

On that thought, Bea felt her own hand close tightly on the head of Mr. Salty's hefty wooden cane, her mind now feverishly in contemplation of the moment of Roy's deliverance. Poor Roy, she thought as she ducked behind a mail receptacle just as Roy stopped. She crouched behind it as he began to turn, so that she felt certain that he did not now see her, despite the fact that Mr. Salty's black top hat was admittedly rather large and perhaps did in fact rise above the top of the receptacle. But then, so what, Bea thought. So what if a big peanut was following him? What did that prove? And besides, should he actually come toward her, Bea already had devised an emergency plan. She would simply turn and run! That would work perfectly, she thought with certainty. For who in his right mind would chase a huge peanut down Fifth Avenue? Nobody, Bea decided, as Roy now shook his head slightly and resumed his northward trudge, nobody, that's who.

Charlie Moon

Charlie found Harry and Cheekie exactly where he expected, slumped in the far corner at the back of Smith's, Harry with head bowed, Cheekie forever looking for a big guy to pick a beef with.

"Gentlemen," Charlie said as he pulled in beside Cheekie. "How they hanging?"

Cheekie's eyes narrowed. "I hear Vandameer is big."

"They don't come any bigger," Charlie declared. "Right, Harry?"

"Big," Harry muttered.

"So here's the deal," Charlie said. "We have a girl who didn't meet her boyfriend. She didn't go back home, and she hasn't checked in since she disappeared. So, what that says to me is, maybe we got a girl who either ran away or was snatched."

"By the big guy?" Cheekie asked, his eyes gleaming hopefully.

"By parties unknown," Charlie answered. "But I got a lead. A guy named Roy Bumble. Works at the Sherry-Netherland. Should be at work later today. I saw him jawing with the missing girl outside the Plaza just a few minutes before she disappeared."

"He a big guy?" Cheekie asked.

"I don't know," Charlie said, a tad irritably. "But if he's not to your liking, Cheekie, I'll set you up with a metal fan."

Cheekie frowned. "Last time somebody wised off to me," he said proudly, "I went to the frigging hospital for three weeks."

Charlie shook his head. "Anyway, this guy's supposed to show up for work at four this afternoon," he said, now returning his attention to Harry. "So, I want you to go over to the Sherry-Netherland and check him out, then get back to me with what you find." He glanced left, right, and behind, then leaned forward. "If this is a kidnapping, and we get this girl back home safe, I don't have to tell you what it means."

"What's it mean?" Harry asked.

"Dough, and plenty of it," Charlie said. "Repeat."

"Bumble," Harry said. "Sherry-Netherland."

Charlie smiled. "Harry, you got a mind like a bear trap."

"Bear," Cheekie muttered disdainfully. "I ain't afraid of no frigging bear."

Roy Bumble

Manhattan was weird, Roy decided.

In Manhattan a guy could be followed by a peanut.

But weirder still was where Roy now found himself. He was actually standing at the front counter of Petrossian, listening in amazement as Allison rattled off what she wanted, jumping to the top of the price-list, ordering what Allison called "tons and tons" of Tsar Imperial Beluga Caviar that, according to the afore-mentioned list, came in at just under a hundred and twenty bucks an ounce.

"I haven't decided where the luncheon will be held," Allison declared to yet another "specialist" with a play-ful toss of her radiantly blond hair. "Perhaps the Metropolitan Club. Or the grand ballroom at the Waldorf." She whipped out the now familiar Platinum Amex. "You'll be calling my father to confirm the order, yes?"

The specialist nodded. "Of course."

Allison smiled, turned briskly and escorted Roy out of Petrossian, the two of them now standing in the mid-morning crowds at 58th and Seventh. She drew in a wild, expansive breath, then turned to Roy. "You can't have a wedding without flowers." She smiled. "There's a shop a few blocks from here that specializes in very rare ones." Her blue eyes turned lethal. "Sooooooooo expensive." She glanced at her watch. "Tiffany should be phoning my father about the bill for the invitations about now."

Roy swallowed hard. "What do you think he'll do?" he asked.

Arthur Vandameer

Arthur felt the brick drop from his rectum and crash with a deafening bang to the floor. "Peacock feathers?" he cried.

"Of course," the voice at the other end replied.

"When did she do this?"

"That would have been about an hour ago, sir."

"So she was there, right in front of you?"

"Yes, sir."

"And you're sure it was Allison?"

"I am," the voice said. "She was last with your wife, Diana, I believe."

Last with your wife Diana, Arthur smoldered, the vision now fully formed in his mind, Diana in her new fur coat, gnawing the head off a seal pup while demonstrating just how much money could be spent between the first sinking of her fangs and the moment the aforementioned pup actually expired.

"Was Allison alone?" he asked politely.

"No, sir."

"Was the guy with her . . . was his name . . . Goonie?"

"Goonie, sir?"

"Could you describe the person or persons who accompanied her?"

"A man," the voice said. "Middle-aged."

A man? Arthur thought. Middle-aged? "Did you notice anything about him?" he asked.

"No," the voice answered reluctantly.

"But he was middle-aged, you're sure?"

"Yes."

"And he was definitely with Allison?"

"They came in and left together, sir."

"Thank you," Arthur said as he returned the phone to the cradle. A man, he mulled, middle-aged. Who could that be? He mulled yet more, and as he mulled, the separate strands of his vast paranoia suddenly wound together in a plot that now seemed perfect for his undoing, Allison clearly in league with the one man in New York who had both the desire and the power to destroy him.

Charlie Moon, Arthur concluded darkly, *the double-crossing rat.*

PART V

THE PLOT QUICKENS

THE EMPEROR
KNEW CLOVIS

Arthur sat in his office at WNIN and considered what he might do before the fated hour of eight p.m., Eastern Standard Time, when the lights would go up, the count ends, all the relevant switches turn, and at that instant, WNIN would broadcast the startling image of himself and Goonie Castillo de la Mancha Diaz into—count 'em—eight million homes.

The surreal nature of that image sank deeper and deeper into Arthur's mind. Goonie in the very chair in which the suitably pin-striped keister of the Chairman of the World Bank had rested only twenty-four hours before. In fact, Arthur calculated, the asses of hundreds of celebrities and world figures had spread out across that fabled chair. No doubt about it, that chair had been the temporary repository of some seriously world-class buttocks, and Arthur simply could not imagine the denim-clad posterior of Goonie Castillo de al Mancha Diaz ever snuggling on to the polished wood that had actually supported the derriere of . . . MY GOD! MADONNA!

For a moment, Arthur imagined the opening lines of the interview:

AV: So, you're Goonie.

Goonie: Well, DUH! (Goonie Full Stop) Even I know that!

Arthur shook his head violently as the interview continued to play in his mind:

Goonie on National Affairs, sagely observing that America is really big and that lots of people live here.

Goonie on World Affairs, giving the same opinion, only shrewdly noting that the world is even bigger with even more people though they didn't really count because he didn't know them.

Goonie on. . . .

Oh why go on, Arthur thought with a disconsolate wag of the head. Two minutes into the interview and the whole damn country would be laughing . . . ESPECIALLY RUSH LIMBAUGH!

Suddenly Arthur's mind seized. Yes, Rush Limbaugh! That explained everything! It was a right-wing plot. A conspiracy to destroy him! And a very clever one, too. For what better way to destroy Arthur Vandameer than to make him appear ridiculous in, count 'em, eight million homes? And what better way to make him appear ridiculous than to have him actually interview Goonie Diaz on national television? And not only interview him, but do it FROM A LIBERAL PERSPECTIVE. For that was certainly what Roland Fitzwater had in mind. He could see it in his mind, Arthur going on and on about how pleased he was that Goonie Castillo de la Mancha Diaz would soon be a member of his family, a son-in-law no less. And he, Arthur, was supposed to do this wearing a mask of delight, with no hint of condescension toward the aforementioned Goonie, despite the fact that the proposed son-in-law could barely count his toes!

"Dear God," Arthur gasped frantically, the words actually blurted in a frenzied whisper from his now entirely dry mouth. It would be worse than the time he'd actually allowed himself to be interviewed by a Cuban journalist, IN SPANISH, just to prove to the world that Arthur Vandameer was not an English-Only kind of guy. The trouble, then and now, was that Arthur spoke only English, a fact that had been made distressingly clear during the interview when, according to the hysterically laughing Rush Limbaugh, Arthur had informed the listening audience that he had once sold stamps on Jupiter, and that his chief fear in life was that wild donkeys might eat his car.

Oh, Limbaugh had had a field day on that one!

AND IT WAS ABOUT TO HAPPEN AGAIN!

Oh, it was clever all right, Arthur thought, his mind now in full paranoid gallop. And who but one Charles W. Moon could be the author of such a plot to destroy him, not through blackmail or extortion or some other more blatant means, but simply by creating the circumstances under which he, Arthur Vandameer, the Voice of American Liberalism, would destroy himself, and not only destroy himself, but do it in full view of the entire nation ON HIS OWN FRIGGING SHOW!

Suddenly the conspiracy took a heady turn, and now, with chilling clarity, Arthur realized that to pull off this fiendish plot, Charlie Moon had to be in league with a co-conspirator who occupied a position on the media food-chain that was much higher than the lowly Moon, himself. Higher even than Arthur. So high, in fact, that there could be no one higher, a man so powerful he could dictate both the form and the hour of Arthur's destruction: in this case the summarily retitled *Left of Mental* . . . at 8pm . . . tonight!

In other words, ROLAND FITZWATER.

For a moment, Arthur's mind flamed with a vision of Moon and Fitzwater, both clad in Roman togas, whispering to each other on the steps of the Forum, plotting the murder of Caesar, daggers in hand, but this time, a murder that would not involve the emperor's actual death, not death by knife wound, but death—slow and agonizing, lasting a full sixty minutes of living color television time—by humiliation.

On a wave of cold panic, Arthur lifted to his feet, whirled around to face the window and looked down to the roiling streets below, a city that suddenly teemed with grinning conspirators. They were everywhere, it seemed, all of them plotting his demise, as well as that of the noble causes he so passionately espoused.

That's it, Arthur thought, a hint of martyrdom now wafting into his consciousness, a Vast Right-Wing Conspiracy!

Suddenly he felt himself emboldened. He was not just fighting for Arthur Vandameer anymore, nor even for his TV show. Oh no, he was fighting for those ideals without which the Republic would surely become, well, Republican. That's why the Charlie Moons of this world were out to get him. *And as for*

Roland Fitzwater, Arthur thought with a cunning and self-congratulatory smile that gave no hint of the senseless and wholly unintelligible simile that suddenly popped into his mind, *he was like a hawk in the thresher, ready for a pruning.*

DANGEROUS INTERROGATIVES

Roy Bumble

Roy Bumble sat at the Roy Rogers on Fifth Avenue, watching the rather large peanut that was seated only a few tables away, and wondered where he really stood now with Allison.

A few minutes before, he'd left the aforementioned Allison on the Bridal Floor at Bergdorf's where, within a few minutes, she'd run through an assortment of bridal gowns, dismissed them all as "ready-made," then summoned yet another specialist from whom she hoped to acquire the name of a "really top designer."

"What I want," she'd told the specialist, "is that Princess Di look."

Evidently the really top designer had been located having lunch at Le Cirque, a repast he'd happily foregone after being informed that the proposed gown would be for the daughter of Arthur Vandameer and that "price was no object."

At that point, Allison had told Roy he might well prefer to have his own lunch now, which had immediately summoned Roy Rogers to Roy Bumble's mind, mainly because he could enjoy an unlimited supply of pickles at the Fixin's Bar.

Now taking a final moment to savor the delectable tang of a final wedge of that very pickle, Roy shifted his eyes from the seemingly ubiquitous peanut that now sat slumped and breathing heavily a few tables distant, and contemplated yet again exactly where he stood with Allison.

The problem, he concluded, was that the plot had changed.

The original plot, Roy recalled, was that Allison would pose as a runaway. Her father would offer a reward. Roy would "find" Allison after a suitable passage of time. Roy would then claim the reward.

This was as far as Roy himself had carried the story forward, though in subsequent conversations, Allison had moved the plot along at least as far as her acceptance of the Best Director Award for her ground-breaking film, *Angles*.

But the plot had changed, and with a peremptory swallow of pickle, Roy meditated on the way the story was now configured.

Number One: Allison's father did not consider her a runaway.

Number Two: Allison's father had offered no reward.

Taken together Roy was forced to admit that these abrupt and thoroughly unanticipated alterations of course had gravely undermined the earlier scheme, and by doing so, now mitigated against his ever receiving the six-figure income he had ardently hoped not to declare on the current year's tax form.

So the problem was how to get the six figures back in the deal.

Roy gloomily surveyed what remained of his earlier pillage of the Fixin's Bar: bits of iceberg lettuce, a few circles of withered onion, a scattering of curiously anemic tomatoes, along with the small piece of metal he'd found nestled among the pickles, though not in time to prevent what his probing tongue now told him was certainly a chipped tooth.

All right, he told himself, think!

And so Roy dropped his head, closed his eyes . . . and thought.

But as always, this was a rather nebulous process, with clouds quickly obscuring other clouds, the whole ponderous labor of cogitation resembling nothing so much as a long crawl through a thick coastal fog, and which, as always, ended with Roy lifting his head from his hands and staring blankly at . . . in this case . . . an enormous peanut that, he vaguely sensed, was also staring back at him.

Bea Bumble

Bea Bumble could not imagine the torment her husband Roy was going through. And despite the fact that the heat was only increasing inside the seemingly hermetically sealed Mr. Salty peanut suit, she allowed herself a moment of sympathy for her deeply vexed husband.

And why shouldn't he be troubled, Bea asked herself, considering his situation. For here Roy was, so magnetically attractive that this little slut was doing everything she could to get her fingers where they shouldn't be, and here Roy was, trying to resist the little slut's imminent and aforementioned fingerings. Other men would have crumbled in an instant, Bea knew, but Roy was holding out, a process that was clearly taking its toll, however. She could see the price in the way Roy had suddenly dropped his head into his hands, held it there for a time, then lifted it again, his face now wreathed in what looked like the aftermath of a terrible headache. A really terrible headache. As a matter of fact, she realized, Roy hadn't looked this distressed since the time he'd tried to install a motorized tie-rack and nearly lost a finger.

Speaking of fingers, Bea thought impatiently, why hadn't the little slut showed up yet? After all, it wasn't getting any cooler inside the peanut suit, and since she'd followed Roy into Roy Rogers, a modest enterprise whose air conditioning unit was clearly on the blink, she'd not even had the occasional relief of a small exterior breeze.

So, where was that little slut, Bea wondered, her impatience only increasing as the furnace in which she was presently encased seemed suddenly to jerk into high gear, sweat now running down her face in such steadily flowing rivulets that she half-expected it to puddle at her feet.

Then, suddenly, she was there.

None other than the little slut, prancing through the door and waving her arm, Roy instantly rising, along with herself in peanut form, so that within a few moments she was on the street again, trudging heavily behind as Roy and the little slut now headed south down Fifth Avenue, the little slut gesticulating madly in that little sluttish way of hers, until she led the clearly tormented Roy toward the welcoming doors of Bulgari where, as Bea noticed from the display in the window, really excellent costume jewelry was in short supply.

Charlie Moon

Charlie Moon glanced at his watch. One-thirty. Still a whole afternoon to go before he'd get word from Harry Stumbo, and perhaps, on that basis, move a step forward in tracking down Allison Vandameer.

Allison Vandameer, Charlie thought, the name itself was frigging gold!

Allison Vandameer.

Only daughter of Arthur Vandameer.

Arthur Vandameer, the world's screwiest pinko-commie fruitcake.

Arthur Vandameer, who would owe Charles W. Moon plenty if the aforementioned Moon found the even earlier aforementioned Allison.

And what, Charlie asked himself with a sparkling shiver of sadistic delight (despite his anticipation of a cruelly lagging preposition) should the pound of Vandameer's flesh consist of? He knew he'd have to get some cash because he'd have to pay Harry and Cheekie both for their services in locating Allison, and in order to ensure they kept their mouths shut, a problem less formidable in the former than the latter, but a problem nonetheless.

But beyond money, what?

Charlie contemplated the delightful catalogue of demands he could make of Arthur Vandameer once he'd delivered his lovely daughter back into his care.

Townhouse?

Charlie liked his crib on Jones Street.

New car?

Who needs a car in Manhattan?

A job?

The one he had was perfect, and with the Vandameer exclusive, it would always be secure.

So what did Charlie want from Arthur Vandameer?

The idea emerged with such lightning speed, he knew it had to be right.

He wanted a frigging apology is what he wanted.

He wanted Arthur Vandameer to apologize to the whole aggrieved nation for the madcap left-wing bull-crap he'd been spewing into their homes for the last thirty years. An apology for the nutty political positions that had resulted in rampant street crime and the collapse of the public schools, swelling welfare rolls and an eviscerated CIA, a whole great nation that would have surely gone down the collective tube had it not been for the common sense of the American people and the titanic figure of Ronald Reagan.

Ah yes, Charlie thought with flaming anticipation of Vandameer's stone-faced apologia, Charlie's own mind now reaching that boiling point from which had spewed his advocacy of such home security devices as guillotine window guards and the use of tactical nuclear weapons on rap concerts. Ah yes, Charlie thought, a damn apology was what he would demand of Arthur Vandameer, and if he didn't get it. . . .

He was busily contemplating the nature of his delicious retaliation should Arthur Vandameer offer the slightest resistance to his entirely just demand when Boy Wonder suddenly appeared at his door, a small square of paper dangling gingerly from his recently manicured fingers.

"Have you seen this?" Boy Wonder asked.

"As of yet," Charlie said, stating what seemed obvious, "I have not."

Boy Wonder placed the paper on Charlie's desk. "It's a fax from WNIN," he said. "Evidently, Arthur Vandameer is going to have a very special show this evening."

Charlie glanced at the paper, which was in fact printed on the WNIN letterhead, and did, in fact, state in the simplest terms that Arthur Vandameer would have a very special show this very evening.

"Arthur Vandameer will have a very special show this evening," Charlie read, thus completing the full body of the text. He looked up from the paper but gave no hint to Boy Wonder of the terrible veil of dread he'd just felt settle over him, the horrible sense—mixed-colloquially speaking—that Arthur Vandameer had an ace down his trousers.

"So?" Charlie said lightly.

"Do you think Vandameer is going to make some sort of . . . announcement?" Boy Wonder probed.

Charlie faked astonishment. "My God, do you suppose he's gay?"

Boy Wonder snapped the paper from Charlie's hand. "What I suppose, Charles, is that this scoop of yours may well have already been scooped."

Charlie sat back in his chair, folded his arms over his chest and pretended a confidence whose roots were currently sunk firmly in mid-air. "He gave me an exclusive," he said. "He can't scoop my scoop."

Boy Wonder eyed Charlie suspiciously. "Has Vandameer called you yet?"

"Yes," Charlie answered.

"So the penny has dropped?" Boy Wonder further inquired. "He knows precisely who you are? THE Charlie Moon who once called him a "platitudinous plug of pusillanimous passivity?'"

"I did?" Charlie asked.

"When he came out against bombing Canada."

"Canada?"

"Which bombing you had advocated because our neighbor to the north was sheltering war resisters."

Charlie nodded. "I was overwrought," he explained. "I'd had the same head cold for a month."

"Be that as it may," Boy Wonder steamed on. "You should be aware that you have promised me a scoop, and that I therefore expect it to be delivered."

"Of course," Charlie said, now trying to conceal the enormous knot that had suddenly knotted in his throat.

Boy Wonder gazed at him sternly. "If you fail to do thus, Charles, be advised that the consequences will be severe."

Charlie suddenly envisioned Jenny Cattrell receiving the Pulitzer Prize, marrying Arthur Vandameer, then moving into the aforementioned Vandameer's palatial Connecticut estate where he, Charlie, would be both currently and forever employed as a mattress pounder.

"Of course," Charlie repeated, the first horrible vision now receding, though only to be replaced by another similarly bleak glimpse into the future, Charlie still toiling on the Vandameer-Cattrell estate, but now as the designated expert on house mites.

"So we understand each other?" Boy Wonder inquired.

"We do," Charlie said with a large, wholly false grin, "I have to deliver the scoop."

Very special show, Charlie thought as Boy Wonder turned briskly and fled the room, *now what might that be*? He sat back in his chair and frantically tried to see into Arthur Vandameer's twisted mind.

Various scenarios emerged, all of them involving Vandameer staring straight into the camera as he made an announcement whose content Charlie fully expected to find egregiously painful.

AV: *Ladies and Gentleman, I'm pleased to announce that following long days of screaming agony, Charles W. Moon has died of a rectal itch.*

Though Charlie had to admit that this was a problem not unknown to him—especially in the early hours—he doubted that Vandameer had actually talked to Dr. Hyman Shapiro, Proctologist to the Stars, or that the aforementioned doctor would have disclosed such otherwise private information without being paid his usual tidy sum.

AV: *Ladies and Gentleman, I'm pleased to announce that the Supreme Court has ruled it unconstitutional for any American to marry within his own ethnic or religious group, and that all such pre-existing unions are hereby annulled.*

Although Charlie had no doubt that Vandameer would welcome such a ruling, he doubted that the High Court, as presently constituted, would look favorably on such government intrusion into matrimonial matters.

AV: *Ladies and Gentlemen, I'm pleased to announce that American military training will henceforth entirely consist of sticking flowers in rifle barrels.*

Charlie shook his head, now determined to speculate on matters less politically charged but more to the point of Charles W. Moon finding employment in some place other than the Vandameer-Cattrell Estate.

All right, he thought, think.

And so he did.

But to no avail.

The problem?

He had not the slightest idea what Arthur Vandameer had up his sleeve, and that, precisely, was what he needed to know. He glanced out the window, where, clearly visible below, he could see the WNIN zipper flowing smoothly.

Which, suddenly made everything clear:

1) Arthur Vandameer worked for WNIN, the only network willing to give the aforementioned Vandameer a platform from which to spew his crack-pot ideas.
2) WNIN had faxed a press release to Boy Wonder which alerted him to the fact that this very evening Vandameer was going to have a "very special show."
3) WNIN and Vandameer were WORKING TOGETHER!
4) The whole thing was a Vast Left-Wing Conspiracy!

And so, Charlie thought with typical Shakespearean aplomb, to horse!

PAC-MAN FOREVER!

Goonie

"This is the Green Room, my boy," Roland Fitzwater said with an expansive wave of his arm.

Well DUH! Goonie thought as his eyes scanned the pale green walls of the aforementioned Green Room.

"All Arthur's guests take a breather here before they come out to be interviewed," Fitzwater added with a wide smile. "Some of the world's most famous people have sat in this room."

Goonie glanced about, his mind—unusual for him—actually managing to contain two thoughts at the same time:

1) Where do they keep the costumes?
2) Where do they keep the bull balls?

Goonie briefly considered making those very inquiries to Fitzwater, but decided that Fitzwater would probably give him the low-down in time. After all, you had to be dressed up right before you went wherever he was going, and the bull balls had to be put in tubs or plates or wrapped up in sacs, the way they'd been before the people on *Fear Factor* had gobbled them.

One question was even more important however.

"Where's the crapper?" Goonie asked.

Fitzwater stared at him silently.

"You know," Goonie explained. "Where you . . . crap."

Fitzwater remained silent for a moment, his eyes blinking slowly. Then, suddenly, he burst out laughing. "Oh, that's rich, son," he cried as his arm swept over Goonie's shoulder. "The crapper is where you crap." He bellowed again. "Down the hall, son. First door on your right." He winked broadly. "And believe me, a lot of world-class celebrities have occupied that seat, too."

Well DUH, Goonie thought as he made his way toward the door Fitzwater now indicated with a flourish, and in which, given the old guy's weirdness, Goonie fully expected to find a room full of famous people either sitting silently, as he imagined Allison must, or thunderously breaking wind . . . like Javiar.

Arthur Vandameer

Arthur Vandameer the Great!

So Arthur Vandameer considered Arthur Vandameer as he squarely faced the carved wooden doors of Madelyn Boyd's imperial digs.

Hercules had never more marveled at his strength, nor Odysseus at his travels, nor the American Bar Association at Bill Clinton's word choice than Arthur Vandameer now marveled at his unwavering determination to meet the Vast Right-Wing Conspiracy eye to eye . . . and wrestle it to the ground.

Rap, rap went Arthur's knuckles against the solid gate.

Silence.

Rap, rap.

And it opened to reveal a not in the least amused Madelyn Boyd, her hair in disarray, a third and this time shimmering blue kimono now wrapped around her seemingly inexhaustible physique.

"These sudden manifestations, Arthur, are becoming a nuisance," Madelyn declared in a tone that, had Arthur been given to vulgar speech, he would have described as "pissy."

"No doubt," Arthur said. "But I have important business."

Madelyn did not appear particularly indulgent of whatever grave matters Arthur had in mind.

"You might say it's a matter of . . ." Arthur stopped, now laboring to define exactly what sort of gravity might induce the aforementioned Madelyn to swing wide the door.

National Security?

If the nation wished to be secure, Madelyn would no doubt declare, it should have closed the borders in 1776.

Economic security?

How could the nation be economically secure, Madelyn would rhetorically inquire, when it had not wisely invested in guaranteed interest-bearing accounts whose numbers were kept secret from all save the nation's mean-faced little Pekinese?

And so it would go, Arthur realized, until the only workable answer suddenly occurred to him.

"I know he's been here," Arthur said.

Madelyn Boyd looked at Arthur disagreeably. "He?"

Arthur smiled. "Roland Fitzwater," he said, then on a wave of pure bravado, he rushed past the aforementioned Madelyn, whirled left at the living room, marched with manly carriage to the bedroom, thrust open the door, and. . . .

"My God," he said, aghast.

"Well, what did you expect, Arthur," Madelyn demanded as she joined him at the entrance to her much-utilized boudoir, "entering unasked."

Harry Stumbo

Harry Stumbo settled into position just across the street from the Sherry-Netherland Hotel. Cheekie stood beside him, scanning the crowd for big guys to stare down, clearly disappointed by the anemic offerings currently provided by the pedestrian traffic, old guys, middle-aged guys, but worse, almost all of them smallish, dressed in suits, not the type who could inflict really serious damage.

"That Javiar," he cooed nostalgically, "He could really toss a guy."

Harry continued to observe the elegant entrance to the Sherry-Netherland, along with the equally elegant

neighborhood that surrounded it, not at all like Times Square, but that was okay with Harry, since the East Side had never been dark and seedy. That was the problem, he thought bitterly, Times Square HAD CHANGED.

"Crap," Harry muttered.

Cheekie looked at him quizzically.

"Change," Harry said sadly.

"Yeah," Cheekie agreed. "It sucks."

For a time, the two men stood silently, watching the street, Harry gloomily running through the list of how many of the old bars had closed, how many had been spruced up, Smith's emerging at the end of his calculations.

"Smith's," he said glumly.

Cheekie nodded.

"Change," Harry repeated

Cheekie shrugged. "It sucks," he said, his gaze now fixed on a delivery van that had just pulled up in front of the Sherry-Netherland.

"It's blocking my view, that van," Cheekie said, his eyes twinkling suddenly as the driver emerged, a man whose arms hung from his shoulders in rippling coils of rock-hard muscle.

"Big," Harry said.

Cheekie grinned happily as he edged away from the building. "Think I'll have a word with him," he said, then headed toward the van, his voice pealing loudly across the busy street, "Hey, butterball, wife got over that little bout of rabies yet?"

Roy Bumble

"Have you noticed," Roy asked as his eyes settled on the far side of the Central Park Roller Skating Rink, "that peanut?"

Allison stared across the rink to where, in the distance, she saw an enormous Mr. Salty Peanut slumped exhaustedly behind the iron rail, his monocled gaze clearly aimed in her direction.

"What about it?" she asked.

"It's been following us," Roy said.

"Following us?" Allison inquired doubtfully.

"All day," Roy said.

Allison frowned. "You didn't tell me you had this little problem," she said.

"Problem?" Roy asked.

"Paranoia," Allison said. "From the Greek word for madness."

"Madness," Roy blurted. "You think I'm crazy?"

Allison looked at him sternly. "One of the shots for my film," she said. "It's from the angle of a paranoid. So I know what I'm talking about. You see, a paranoid has a distorted vision of the world. My angle reflects that, and so, in mapping the shot I had to. . . ."

And so and so on, as Allison continued, Roy now trying to look attentive as Allison detailed the "paranoid angle," but all the time glancing back across the rink to where Mr. Salty slumped, facing him so blatantly, and with such fierce determination to record each and every movement, that suddenly, everything Allison had just told him made perfect sense.

He was paranoid!

This whole scheme was making him paranoid.

So much so, that at this very moment, Roy wondered if perhaps concealed in the dark interior of the peanut suit was none other than Arthur Vandameer or, more likely, the private detective he'd hired to track his beloved daughter down.

"Maybe it's . . ." he sputtered.

"It's what?" Allison inquired, with unconcealed irritation at having been abruptly interrupted in her admittedly lengthy description of the paranoid angle.

"The peanut."

Allison looked at him crossly.

"Maybe it works for your father."

"My father?" Allison asked.

"Maybe he hired a private detective," Roy explained. "To find you. And maybe the detective dressed up like a . . . peanut?"

Allison's eyes narrowed. "Paranoid," she repeated.

Roy shook his head. She was right. He was going crazy! He was losing his mind! Nothing like this had happened when he'd cut the heads off parking meters or unloaded Sal Pallucci's Ford Explorer. And the only reason it was happening now, Roy realized, was because he was actually playing in the big league, actually pulling a scam on a Big Somebody, a guy who lived in Manhattan.

AND IT WAS SCARING HIM TO DEATH!

"Allison," he blurted as a terrible wave of anxiety swept over him, "I can't do this. I'm out of my depth, here."

Allison's eyes grew steely. "What's the matter with you?" she cried. "It's just a peanut!"

Roy swallowed hard. "I'm from Queens," he stammered weakly. "I don't belong in this thing. I'm out of my depth is what I'm saying." For a moment, Roy thought he might actually burst into tears. But that would be okay, he reasoned, because he'd soon be doing the same thing as he pled for leniency before he was sentenced to eighty years of hard labor and subsequently became the cowering cell mate and nightly love interest of a guy named Bull Diablo.

Allison Vandameer planted her fist on her right hip and didn't give an inch. "What is it about that peanut?" she demanded.

"It's not just the peanut," Roy whined. "It's that . . . that. . . ."

"What?"

"That I'm small," Roy admitted. "Small-time. And this thing . . . it's . . . it's. . . ."

Allison closed her eyes slowly. "Are you telling me that you don't want to go through with our plan?"

Roy saw the dream of a lifetime fade before his eyes, the Big Scam on a Big Somebody simply dematerialize, a loss of possibility that would leave him forever in . . . well . . . Queens. But what else could he do? He was not a guy who lived in Manhattan, nor even a guy who could run a scam on a guy who lived in Manhattan. He was a guy who lived in Queens and unloaded various items from Sal Pellucci's SUV, items his wife, the wholly immaculate Bea, would not even allow him to unpack. So wasn't he the luckiest guy in the world, he asked himself, to have a wife like Bea? Yes, he decided, now bent upon the straight and narrow. Yes!

"Well?" Allison demanded.

Roy nodded. "I mean . . . I . . . it's just that . . ."

Allison frowned. "Oh all right," she said, now whipping her cell phone from the Gucci bag she'd just purchased, along with a full set of travel luggage, the aforementioned luggage to be shipped directly to the Pierre. "You can call Art," she said as she punched the numbers. "Tell him you found me and that you're bringing me to his office."

"To his office?" Roy asked, cringing visibly.

"He'll probably give you something," Allison said. "It won't be much, but something."

At the moment Roy would have been more than pleased to accept, as a token of Arthur Vandameer's appreciation, a small goldfish in a plastic bag.

"Here," Allison said as she handed Roy the phone. "Tell him we're on our way."

Roy took the phone, listened as it rang repeatedly, then to a voice mail recording.

"He's not in his office," he said as he returned the phone to Allison. He glanced over to where Mr. Salty now began to slump toward the ground, its spindly arms holding briefly to the iron railing before they dropped away as the entire peanut crumpled to the ground. For a moment he thought of mentioning the peanut's sudden and unexpected demise to Allison, but thought it better not to digress from the subject at hand. "Not in his office," he repeated.

"Not in his office," Allison mused.

Roy glanced at his watch. "I have to go to work. What do you want to do?"

"He has a show at eight," Allison said. "We can't miss him at that point."

This sounded perfectly reasonable to Roy. "Where do you want to meet?"

"The Sherman statue," Allison said.

This also sounded perfectly reasonable to Roy. "All right," he said.

"He's always at his office before the show," Allison said, almost to herself. She stared out over the verdant reaches of Central Park. "I wonder where he could be?"

Arthur Vandameer

Arthur surveyed the assorted detritus of Roland Fitzwater's most recent leave-taking.

"He got a call and had to leave quickly," Madelyn explained.

"So it seems," Arthur said, trying very hard not to add a triumphant grin as he did a rough calculation of what his former protector and now determined nemesis had left behind.

A toy wheelbarrow to whose handles three brightly colored helium filled balloons had been attached.

A bubble machine which even now, a full two hours after Roland's departure, still managed to lift a few limp bubbles into the strangely buttery air.

A large black and white blow-up of the set of Romper Room mounted on a wooden easel.

A purple Slinky.

"A purple Slinky?" Arthur inquired.

"Don't ask," Madelyn replied sourly. "So, Arthur, what do you intend to do with this . . . information?"

Arthur resisted the impulse to tell Madelyn that he envisioned nothing less that the salvation of the

Republic, and instead replied, "Use it to sobering effect."

"That, Arthur, is not an answer," Madelyn said, "But I do have your assurance, do I not, that the name Madelyn Boyd will not appear in your commentary?"

"It will not," Arthur assured her. He peered about the room. "Purple Slinky?" he asked.

Madelyn frowned. "The precise meaning of these . . . curiosities has never been divulged to me," she said.

"You don't mind being thus unenlightened?"

"Do you think if I actually knew it would enhance the experience?" Madelyn asked sharply.

"And just how long have you been seeing Roland?" Arthur asked.

"A number of years," Madelyn answered without the least sense of having kept Arthur rather profoundly outside the loop.

"So, the entire time I was also seeing you, you were also seeing Roland?"

"That would be the inference."

"But why?"

Madelyn made no attempt to sugarcoat her reasoning. "Well, as you know, Arthur, you have always been somewhat . . . sporadic?"

Arthur felt himself color. "Well, at least I never required Slinkys."

"I wouldn't care if you'd needed two ponies and an ink blotter," Madelyn said. "The point is to. . . ."

"Yes, yes," Arthur interrupted. He once again surveyed the room, now wondering in precisely what way he might use the knowledge he'd so recently acquired concerning the curious erotics of one Roland Fitzwater to hammer the aforementioned Fitzwater into leaving his show the hell alone.

1) He could threaten to hand it over to a rival network.
2) He could threaten to hand it over to a hostile journalist.
3) He could threaten to hand it over to Mrs. Roland Fitzwater.
4) He could threaten to divulge the aforementioned erotics on the recently retitled *Left of Mental*.

Briefly, Arthur considered the juicy format of such a program, saw himself in his usual chair, and on the other side, none other than Dr. Joyce Brothers, the table which separated them now generously supplied with the very articles that were at this precise moment still gathered in and around the bed of Madelyn Boyd.

AV: *So, tell me, Dr. Brothers, what is your interpretation of, say . . . that purple Slinky?*

The moment provided Arthur with such a feeling of delightful power, he very nearly lifted his fist into the air and yelled, YES!

"So," he said, his gaze now focused coolly on the increasingly steamed features of Madelyn Boyd. "I suppose . . . I'll be . . . seeing . . . you. . . ?"

"I think not," Madelyn responded crisply.

This, Arthur realized, was a price he had not expected to pay in his struggle to save the Republic. "You mean . . . ?" he stammered, his eyes, despite the effort, widening in shock. "You mean. . . ."

"I mean you will not be receiving any additional favors, Arthur," Madelyn told him sternly.

With that, she turned, and marched to the beautifully carved front door, where she remained a few seconds later when Arthur at last joined her there.

"But Madelyn," he began, his once heroic voice now reduced to a gentle whine, "You're dismissing me entirely?"

"I am."

"But so fast?"

"This is New York, Arthur," Madelyn said. "Everything moves fast."

"But . . ."

Madelyn threw open the door. "Fast, Arthur," she reiterated firmly, "The epilogue comes in forty minutes."

Charlie Moon

Charlie couldn't believe his own eyes. Here he was, perched beneath the scrolling zipper of WNIN, wondering just what sort of ruse he might use to get past a security system that would have given pause to a cruise missile, when, out of the blue, there was the only proof he needed that he was being set up.

Not just Roland Fitzwater, complete with his characteristic white cowboy hat and a silver belt buckle bright enough to blind the Persian cavalry. Not only the aforementioned Fitzwater, but loping at his side, loping in such simian posture, his knuckles all but dragging the ground over which he lumbered, a youth dressed in complete hip-hop attire, his pants only covering his backside because gravity lacked the power to do more, sneakers the size of gunboats, their laces flopping about like dying tapeworms, a baseball cap appropriately reversed, a t-shirt emblazoned with the chivalrous advice, SHUT UP BITCH!, all of this speaking as one the name of the previously referenced youth, that is to say: GOONIE!

At that moment, as Charlie observed, this otherwise unlikely pair was making its way from Fitzwater's impressive limousine to the imposing glass doors of WNIN, a distance Charlie calculated as no more than thirty yards, thus traversable in mere seconds, a fact that made it clear to Charlie that he had to think pretty damn fast!

There had to be a way, he thought, a way to get inside the building, get a look inside Vandameer's office, get a handle on what he and Fitzwater were cooking up, find out by what dire and dreadful means they were conspiring to destroy him.

He glanced up at the zipper, which at that moment was giving the ever-increasing death-toll of yesterday's Polynesian tidal wave, and wondered exactly how he could approach the curious pair that had, by then, covered half the distance from the limo to the imposing glass doors.

His thoughts ran—to use an expression beloved by Boy Wonder—thusly:

1) He could faint.
2) He could approach Fitzwater and reveal that he had "certain information" concerning Arthur Vandameer.
3) He could approach Fitzwater and reveal that he had "certain information" concerning the whereabouts of Allison Vandameer.
4) He could approach Fitzwater and say that he had nude photographs of...well, anybody!

The problem with three of the foregoing four approaches, Charlie quickly concluded, was that he had no such "certain information" and that the only nude photos currently in his possession were securely locked in the bottom drawer of his bedroom bureau. From this unfortunate truth, Charlie wisely concluded that three of the aforementioned four approaches would not prove useful, thus leaving him but one option.

And so, arms lifting widely and with buckling knees, Charlie fainted.

Roy Bumble

Roy saw it immediately.

Fydor Potanovich was in no mood for bullcrap.

Roy knew this not only because he, Roy, was highly observant, a man who could divine the inner lives and ever fluctuating sensibilities of other human beings, but because Fydor's initial greeting had revealed the most subtle calibrations of his, Fydor's, momentarily unguarded mood.

"Where the hell you been, asshole?" Fydor judiciously inquired.

Roy thought fast, but not fast enough. "Uh," he said, then let his astonishingly detailed reply wither in the air.

"You're twenty minutes late, Roy," Fydor boomed, thus revealing yet another downward shift of his volatile inner barometer.

"Uh," Roy repeated . . .

"Well?"

"I . . . was . . . uh . . ."

"Yeah?"

"Uh . . ."

Fydor thumbed the side of the large metal timeclock that hung beside him. "Twenty damn minutes, Roy."

"Uh," Roy speedily replied. "I was. . . ."

"Was what?" Fydor wished to know.

"I was. . . ." Roy weighed the possibility that Fydor might actually believe that he'd been abducted by aliens, decided that he probably wouldn't, and so decided on a more plausible reason for his apparent tardiness, ". . . hit by a meat wagon."

Plausible as Roy knew this excuse to be, since this very circumstance had often hindered his father's timely arrival at the shoe factory in Long Island City, Fydor nonetheless appeared to harbor grave doubts.

"Meat wagon?" Fydor howled. "What you mean, meat wagon?"

"On . . . Fifth Avenue," Roy declared, though he had to admit that as far as he knew there were no meat markets on Fifth Avenue and thus it was an unlikely route by which such wagons might traverse the city.

"Lost," he said, covering this unexpected wrinkle in what had at first seemed an incontestable cover.

"Okay, Roy," Fydor said. "I ain't gonna ask you no more questions." His eyes narrowed menacingly. "A guy, he come look for you."

Roy's felt his heart-muscle spasm. "A guy? Me?"

"He ask about girl. This girl, he tell me she vanish."

"Vanish?" Roy fearfully inquired.

"Vanish," Fydor firmly confirmed.

With that, Fydor whirled around and left Roy to his work, which amounted to very little, merely going up and down in the residential elevator, but nonetheless a job whose complexity required no less than eighty-seven percent of Roy's mental power, and which, at this point he found it difficult to do, since the problem of a "guy" looking for him now demanded an equally large slice of his intellectual acuity.

A guy?

Fydor had given no further description, but Roy was pretty sure he would have mentioned it if the guy had been dressed as a peanut. He eased himself out of the Sherry-Netherland and looked both ways down the street. No peanut. Okay, Roy thought, so it wasn't THAT guy.

For no discernible reason, Roy felt an odd relief, then instantly tensed again, since if it had been a peanut, Fydor would have mentioned it, and so, as night follows day, Roy would have been on alert for a . . . well . . . a peanut.

But since Fydor had not mentioned a peanut, then, well, THE GUY COULD BE ANYBODY!

Again, Roy paused and fearfully glanced both ways down the street. Even one of those guys, he thought, peering across the street to where one guy was helping another guy wrap a large bandage around his head.

Harry Stumbo

Harry tightened the bandage around Cheekie's skull while the aforementioned Cheekie grinned happily.

"How far he toss me, you think?" Cheekie asked.

"Long way," Harry answered.

The blood had stopped flowing from Cheekie's head by then, but the imprint of the hood-ornament upon which it had earlier been dashed was still visible on Cheekie's right cheek.

"Ten feet?" Cheekie inquired, clearly trying to calculate if he'd set a new record for wingless flight. "At least ten, right?"

"Ten," Harry muttered, now lifting Cheekie to his feet.

Cheekie's smile expanded as Harry drew him from the sidewalk. He felt his head, probing the gash beneath the gauze wrapping he always brought with him, and which, after this latest airborne adventure, he'd been more than happy to provide to Harry, who, as Cheekie knew, was by now adept at street-level first aid.

"That's a beaut," Cheekie said. "What do think, couple inches?"

"Couple," Harry said, his attention suddenly drawn to a heavyset, middle-aged man who now stood, peering at him, from the entrance of the Sherry-Netherland.

"And deep," Cheekie added with a sense of triumph. "Maybe a quarter-inch?"

"Maybe," Harry said, his concentration entirely focused on the door of the Sherry-Netherland.

"Man," he said.

Cheekie's eyes sparkled. "Yeah?" he asked excitedly as he turned his gaze toward the hotel. He stared at the man in the uniform for a moment, then said, "You figure that's him, Harry?"

Harry nodded.

Cheekie slapped his hands together. "Let's go get the rat bastard," he snarled eagerly

"Wait," Harry said.

"Why?"

"Watch."

Cheekie shrugged. "Okay," he said, giving in to higher authority, though, as Harry could tell by the self-satisfied grin that suddenly swam onto his face, Cheekie had already decided upon the insult he would offer when the time was right.

TALLYRAND WHO?

Allison Vandameer

Allison took her customary seat a few yards from the imposingly gilded statue of William Tecumseh Sherman. She drew in a deep breath and tallied up the bills that would, by then, be warming the heart of American Express, as well as the various specialists who, by day's end, had doubtlessly made their own calculations, after which, with complete confidence, they'd telephoned various husbands, wives and significant others to convey the glad tidings that already, in mid-summer, they'd not only made their yearly quota of sales, but would incontestably be selected as their particular commercial establishment's (Tiffany, Petrossian, Bergdorf Goodman, et al.) "Specialist of the Year."

Allison smiled at how easy it was to make people happy. All you had to do was bloat the credit card, spend with merciless abandon, truly spread the wealth as, she noted with sadistic pleasure, Arthur was forever advocating in his television commentary, though with, as she equally noted, little attention to spreading the particular wealth that was his own. As a matter of fact,

Arthur was, by all accounts, a notorious spendthrift, a miserly tipper, a man abhorred by waiters, doormen, emergency electricians and locksmiths, along with scores of various delivery people who, after depositing stoves, refrigerators, pianos, or perhaps no more than a large pizza with anchovies and green peppers (Arthur's favorite) were rewarded with such a paltry expression of appreciation that they turned abruptly on their heels and departed the apartment loudly whistling "Hey Big Spender," which, as Allison recalled, was a musical number from the Broadway hit, *Sweet Charity*.

These thoughts returned Allison directly to the matter at hand, and for a moment she reviewed the situation as it had so surprisingly developed during the course of the last twenty-four hours.

First, Goonie had not shown up at the appointed place and hour. He had not shown up for reasons as yet unaccounted for, an absence which, as Allison realized with a sudden distressing urgency, inevitably called into question those irresistibly attractive features which, evidently, Goonie had, in fact, successfully managed to resist . . . or otherwise HE WOULD HAVE BEEN THERE!

This was a chilling thought, and for the first time, Allison felt a quiver of self-doubt. Could it be, she wondered, that her allure was already fading? Several of Arthur's wives had alluded to this very diminution of female power, associated it with time, and applied against it a vast array of oils and powders, ointments and sprays, not to mention some very expensive time beneath the skilled surgical knives of one Dr. Winthrop A. Pasternak, Plastic Surgeon to the Stars. As a matter of fact, Allison recalled, Evelyn Wills, Arthur's second wife, had had her skin stretched so tightly across her skull that it actually squeaked when she turned her head.

Allison discreetly searched her face for signs of incipient drift or sag, decided there were none, and on that thought, returned to the conclusion she'd earlier drawn concerning Goonie's failure to appear, and which now, after this most recent facial check, seemed utterly confirmed, the fact, never in serious doubt, that the aforementioned Goonie was an idiot.

This conclusion did nothing to illuminate the current state of affairs, however, and so Allison immediately concentrated on her current situation.

This current situation presented itself as follows:

1) Goonie had not shown up.
2) Roy Bumble had appeared instead.
3) A mutually beneficial scheme had been hatched by which Allison would pretend to be a runaway, Arthur, desperate to get her back, would offer a reward, which the aforementioned Roy Bumble would collect, and thus Allison would be returned home to a thoroughly chastened Arthur, who would then, in desperation to prevent any future flight from home, give his blessing to her, Allison's, attendance at UCLA School of Film, the alma mater of many famous directors, none of whom had ever, in Allison's estimation, actually used camera angles to portray character.

But the plan had gone awry, as Allison had no choice but to admit. No reward had been offered. Worse, Arthur had actually announced her marriage to Goonie on national television. This was a bluff, of course, but it had worked as far as Roy Bumble was concerned, so that now, here she sat, staring at General Sherman, waiting for Roy Bumble, while, at the perimeter of her vision, a large peanut rounded the far corner of the Plaza Hotel and proceeded toward the statue of General Sherman with all the steely determination of a Rebel charge, then turned abruptly and stormed directly toward Allison like an enraged locomotive, bursts of black smoke all but belching from Mr. Salty's fluttering sides until it screeched to a halt before her and sputtered from its steaming inner depths a single furious interrogative:

"WHERE'S MY ROY?"

"Roy?" Allison inquired.

"WHERE'S MY ROY?"

Allison had never been approached by such a furiously riled peanut, and so took the side of caution. "He went to work," she answered.

"WORK?" the peanut barked.

Allison nodded, then watched as the peanut stormed away, Mr Salty's impressive wooden cane tapping with menacing effect on the concrete walk.

Charlie Moon

It was time, Charlie thought, to come to.

He opened his eyes and stared about, giving no

sense that he recognized the famous face that hung above him.

"Are you all right, boy?" Roland Fitzwater asked.

Charlie moaned softly. "It must be the heat," he said.

"Well, hell yes, son," Fitzwater agreed. He swept off the enormous cowboy hat and vigorously fanned Charlie's face. "That's why I brought you inside here, for the air conditioning."

Charlie glanced about at the array of EMS personnel who were gathered in the sleek marble lobby of WNIN, all of them practically chomping at the bit to gather him up by ankle and shoulder, transfer him to one of at least three awaiting gurneys, and transport him to the nearest hospital.

"I didn't wait for these guys to show up," Fitzwater declared. "I said to myself, 'It's the heat,' and dragged you right inside the lobby here."

"Fast thinking," Charlie whispered. "Thank you, Mr. . . ."

"Fitzwater," Fitzwater said. "Roland Fitzwater." He returned the cowboy hat to his head and thrust out a Texas-sized hand. "Proud to meet you, son."

Charlie forced his eyes to tear with gratitude. "Thank you, Mr. . . . uh...Fitzwater." Laboriously, he made an attempt to rise.

"Okay," Fitzwater said, tucking a second Texas-sized hand beneath Charlie's slumped shoulder. "Ease up."

Thus lifted to his feet, Charlie surveyed the crowded lobby while he searched for the next step in his plan.

And miraculously, the next step appeared.

"Wait a minute," Charlie said as if he'd suddenly been struck by lightening. "You mean you're . . . THE Roland Fitzwater?"

"Himself," Fitzwater said with a broad smile.

"The owner of WNIN?" Charlie asked, his eyes now fixed in beatific wonder.

"The very one, son," Fitzwater confirmed.

"The network that has my favorite show," Charlie continued, his features now masked in baleful longing, "though I've never actually seen it . . . live."

"What show is that, my boy?" Fitzwater inquired.

"*Speaking Truth To Power*," Charlie replied. "With Arthur Vandameer."

Fitzwater's furry eyebrows inched closer together. "You actually like that show, son?" he asked.

"Oh yes," Charlie crowed. "I think Arthur Vandermeer is . . ." He had no choice but finish the sentence with something other than *the largest and most prodigious ass on planet earth*. ". . . so deep."

"Deep?" Fitzwater gasped "Arthur?"

"Deep," Charlie repeated firmly. "A philosopher."

"Philosopher?" Fitzwater laughed. "Arthur?" The laughter turned thunderous. "Oh, that's rich, son." He gave Charlie an affectionate slap on the back, albeit a slap that, despite the affection, thoroughly rattled the aforementioned Charlie's teeth.

"Well, you're in luck, my boy," Fitzwater howled. "Because this very night, Arthur Vandameer is going to have a helluva show."

"Really?" Charlie chirped. "You mean, it's going to be a . . . very special show?"

"You're damn right it is," Fitzwater crowed, his eyes beaming. "And you're gonna to be sitting right there watching it."

"You mean . . . live?" Charlie appeared to lose his footing. "Me?"

"Now don't faint on me again." Fitzwater laughed. He draped his enormous arm over Charlie's shoulder. "Come with me, son. I wanna show you the Green Room."

Harry Stumbo

By the time they reached the door of the Sherry-Netherland, Harry was pretty sure Cheekie had his opening line in place.

He was right.

"That clown suit looks a little tight on you, Bubble-Butt," Cheekie opined as the aforementioned and now seriously undercapitalized Bubble-Butt opened the wide glass door of the Sherry-Netherland.

"Excuse me?" Bubble-Butt asked.

Cheekie cackled. "You deaf, or just stupid?"

Harry placed a restraining hand on Cheekie's shoulder. "Roy Bumble," he said.

"Roy Bumble?" asked Roy Bumble, a.k.a. Bubble-Butt.

"You deaf or just stupid?" Cheekie repeated.

"Roy Bumble," Harry repeated.

"Roy Bumble," Roy Bumble said. "You're looking for Roy Bumble."

"Yeah," Cheekie snapped. "You him, Bubble-Butt?"

"Well . . ." Bubble-Butt began. "I. . . ."

"It's him, Harry," Cheekie laughed. "So, Bubble-Butt, where's the girl?"

"Girl?" Roy asked.

"That's right, girl," Cheekie said. "What's the matter, Queer-Bait, you don't know the difference?"

Queer-Bait appeared quite utterly perplexed.

"Allison Vandameer," Harry offered by way of clarification.

"I don't think this frigging guy knows what a girl is, Harry," Cheekie said with a bright glimmer in his eyes. "Probably goes for them barnyard creatures." He laughed. "Am I right, Goat-Boy?"

Harry shrugged. With aspersions now cast on Roy Bumble's appearance and sexual practices now depleted, he could not imagine what Cheekie might come up with next.

"Or is your right hand named Matilda?" Cheekie laughed.

Harry expected Bumble at last to throw a punch, but instead, a voice shook the air behind him.

"LEAVE MY ROY ALONE!" the voice thundered.

Cheekie whirled around to face a . . . peanut.

"LEAVE MY ROY ALONE," the peanut roared.

Cheekie glanced at Harry.

Harry shrugged.

Cheekie turned back to the . . . peanut? He shifted his weight from foot to foot, opened his mouth, but nothing came out.

"LEAVE MY ROY ALONE," the peanut repeated no less hotly than before, but this time with the added flourish of an impressive wooden cane.

Again Cheekie shifted his weight, and again his mouth opened wordlessly.

"LEAVE MY ROY ALONE!"

Cheekie stared at the peanut as if it were a blank wall he could not get over or through, and Harry could see a horrible frustration rise into his face. For how, after all, could a man insult a . . . peanut?

The peanut raised its cane threateningly. "Scat!"

Cheekie looked as if he'd been hit in the face with a cream pie. "Scat?" he whispered. He looked at Harry pleadingly. "Scat?"

Harry shrugged.

Cheekie returned his gaze to the peanut. "Uh . . . lis . . ."

But clearly the peanut had exhausted its patience, a fact made abundantly clear as the cane fell with a loud crack across Cheekie's head and the aforementioned Cheekie dropped to the sidewalk like a sack of sand.

Then the peanut turned toward Harry. "LEAVE MY ROY ALONE!"

It was a distinctly female voice, and so Harry could offer only a helpless nod in return, since clearly Mrs. Salty's rage was romantically inspired. And faced with love like that, Harry concluded, what else could he do?

PART VI

WHAT IF ALL THE COWS WERE GROWN?
(ANSWER IN PREQUEL)

MISSION
IMPROBABLE

Charlie Moon

Charlie Moon could hardly believe his good fortune. Not only had the faint worked, it had propelled him much deeper into the dark heart of the Vast Left-Wing Conspiracy than he'd have imagined possible when the idea of fainting had first occurred to him.

And if he needed any more proof of the faint's strikingly unexpected effectiveness, he had only to look around him.

For here he was, in the Green Room adjacent to the set of Arthur Vandameer's staggeringly offensive *Speaking Truth to Power*, although, as he'd noticed upon being ushered into the Green Room by none other than Roland Fitzwater, a crew of stage hands had already removed the "T" from "Truth" and the "P" from "Power" in what appeared to be a hurried effort to revamp the entire set of the aforementioned *Speaking Truth to Power*, so that it now looked less like an interview program than an updated version of *The Gong Show*.

But there was something even better than being in close proximity to Arthur Vandameer's curiously remodeled set. Something even better than being in Arthur Vandameer's own Green Room.

Yes! Miracles of miracles, he was in the Green Room WITH GOONIE!

And, yes! Charlie thought as he peered at the young man who slouched gloomily on the Green Room's opposite sofa, this had to be Goonie. For what other young man might he be? On close observation, he appeared to be an "Eskimo"; appeared to be careless of dress, and from the way he'd picked up one of the scores of news magazines which lay about the room, one which, in this case, bore the face of the current Secretary of State, appeared to be about as interested in world affairs as he might have been, say, in the punctilious usage of English grammar. In fact, once in hand, the young man had peered at the aforementioned Secretary as if trying to decipher the occult markings of an Egyptian sarcophagus, then with a look of utter bafflement put it aside. Such dress and attitude, for Charlie Moon, spelled only one thing: G-O-O-N-I-E.

The problem, as Charlie was quick to recognize, was in discovering exactly how Goonie fit into the Vast Left-Wing Conspiracy.

Charlie had no doubt that Goonie had been recruited to play a part in the dastardly plot Arthur Vandameer and Roland Fitzwater were, well, plotting.

But what part?

That was the question.

Charlie decided to make subtle inquiry.

"Hey," Charlie said.

Goonie lifted his eyes from their curiously downward gaze.

"My name's Moon," Charlie said, beaming a smile. "And you are?"

"Uh . . . Joselito," Goonie replied in the suspicious tone of a young man who'd just been approached by a strange man in a raincoat.

"Eee-toe," Charlie said, now trying to impress this Joselito with his, Charlie's, knowledge of diverse cultures, "that means 'little,' right? On the end of a name like that?"

Little Jose appeared unsure, and so Charlie decided on another approach.

"Forgive me for asking," he said, striving mightily to keep a straight face, "But haven't I seen you on TV? You're . . . somebody, right?"

Little Jose again appeared unsure, but Charlie suppressed the impulse to ask if this uncertainty extended to the notion of whether he was animal, mineral, or vegetable.

"The leader of something?" Charlie added with face still straight, although the effort expended in keeping it so was increasing with each question. "A spokesman. You're a spokesman for some cause or something, am I right?"

Goonie looked as if he'd been asked to determine how long it would take Train A, going eighty miles an hour, to overtake Train B, going seventy miles an hour, if Train A were twenty miles behind Train B.

To which question, Charlie now supposed, Goonie would no doubt have answered, "False."

"Okay," Charlie said, now deciding that even the most blatant of deceits would skip lightly over Goonie's head. "Let me ask you directly."

Goonie ducked his head, as if a spear had just been hurled at him by an irate tribesman.

"Why are you here in the Green Room?" Charlie asked.

Goonie looked relieved that the question did not involve diversely speeding trains. "I'm going on the show," he answered.

"The show?" Charlie asked. "Arthur Vandameer's show?"

Goonie nodded.

Charlie could not imagine such a thing. Goonie on *Speaking Truth to Power*, or whatever the rearranged letters would finally title Arthur Vandameer's continuing effort to weaken the social fabric of America. "You're Vandameer's guest?" he asked. "You're going to be . . . interviewed?"

"I guess," Goonie said. His eyes darkened. "But no way I'm gonna eat no bull balls," he declared.

Charlie wondered if he were actually alive or living out some idiotic dream. For a moment he stared at Goonie Castillo de la Mancha Diaz as if he were a phantasm, a weird vision his mind had seized upon to drive him mad.

"You haven't by any chance seen any of the questions Arthur Vandameer is going to be asking you?" he inquired tentatively, like a man poking at a bloated body.

"Questions?" Goonie asked, now clearly roused not

just to attention, but to the first icy ripples of panic. "He's gonna ax me questions?"

"It's an interview show," Charlie explained, barely able to keep the volcanic frustration from his voice. "If you're the guest, then of course he's going to 'ax' you questions."

Goonie's face paled in terror, his mind clearly rushing through the infinite interrogatory possibilities until he appeared at last to seize the one that most locked his heart in dread, "You mean, like . . . capitals and states?"

Charlie felt his brain begin to ache. "Jeez," he moaned just beneath his breath, then reasoned wisely that he had no choice but continue, though clearly down a different road. "Listen, Joselito," he said. "Maybe we could work together on this thing."

Goonie's eyes brightened, a clear indication that Charlie's offer to provide himself as a crib-sheet would not be summarily refused.

Charlie presented a winning smile. "But first, you have to tell me how you actually came to be a . . . guest on Arthur Vandameer's show."

Roy Bumble

Despite the thickness of Mr. Salty's gloves, Roy felt his wife Bea's fingernails press into his fleshy right thigh.

"You gotta come clean, Roy," Bea commanded. "You gotta come clean and say you're sorry."

Roy had been expecting Bea to reach this radically discomfiting conclusion during the whole time he'd related the story of having met Allison at the General Sherman statue, how the aforementioned Allison had, upon the failure of her boyfriend to appear, concocted a scam by which she would pretend to run away, be "found" by Roy, who would be given a reward by Arthur Vandameer, who would then send Allison to UCLA School of Film, after which, she, Allison, would make her ground-breaking movie, *Angles*, for which she would receive the Best Director Award during lavish ceremonies at the Kodak Theater in Los Angeles.

Roy had hoped that Bea's only question would concern the location of the aforementioned Kodak Theater, but instead she'd asked no question at all, but merely issued the demand she now repeated in an even more determined voice.

"You gotta come clean, Roy, and say you're sorry."

Roy swallowed hard. He'd never felt so small. Here he was, a guy who'd dreamed his whole life of pulling a major scam, a scam on Somebody Big, a guy who lived in Manhattan, and by that means himself become Somebody Big, a guy who lived in Manhattan. And then, out of nowhere, the Somebody Big had materialized in the form of none other than Allison Vandameer, daughter of Arthur Vandameer, WHO DEFINITELY LIVED IN MANHATTAN!

And here he was . . . having to come clean and say he was sorry.

But how? Roy wondered.

"But how?" Roy asked.

Bea Bumble's eyes glittered from somewhere among the internal organs of Mr. Salty. "You gotta talk to the guy you was gonna . . ." The word "con" appeared to stick like a chicken bone in Bea Bumble's throat "You got to come clean and tell him you're sorry."

"Tell Arthur Vandameer I'm sorry?" Roy gasped.

"Otherwise you'll always feel guilty," Bea Bumble declared in no uncertain terms, her fingers tightening, as Roy noticed, around Mr. Salty's alarmingly sturdy cane.

He nodded. "Okay," he said. "When?"

Bea Bumble rose in peanut form and cast her gaze down the steadily darkening canyon of Fifth Avenue. "Now," she said.

"But he's about to do his show," Roy protested.

Bea Bumble looked at Roy as if this were but a ruse, a way of avoiding his responsibility to come clean and say he was sorry, which, of course, it was.

"You gotta come clean," Bea Bumble repeated sternly. "And say you're sorry."

"But . . . how will we get in?" Roy whined. "There's got to be a lot of, you know, security."

This problem seemed perfectly real to Roy, but Bea clearly remained unimpressed.

"We'll find a way," she said.

Allison Vandameer

Allison was getting cranky. The city was getting dark, the hour was getting late, her body was getting hungry, and the diamond-studded wristwatch which the specialist at Tiffany had suggested as the perfect accessory for her equally diamond-studded bridal tiara wasn't providing encouraging news. According to the aforementioned diamond-studded wristwatch, the hour had reached just past seven, and here she was, just as the night before, waiting for an unfortunate male, who before the lateness of the hour began to suggest otherwise, she'd considered quite tightly wound around her little finger. And yet this particularly aforementioned male, namely one Roy Bumble, had, for reasons as yet unexplained, thus far failed to show up, a failure to appear that Allison thought might have something to do with a peanut.

But worst of all, as Allison was having an increasingly difficult time keeping secret from the so far blessedly uninformed rush-hour pedestrians who thronged about her, when she got hungry, she got cranky, and when she got cranky . . . she got gas!

I've got to eat! Allison told herself, as she once again successfully suppressed the gravely unpleasant consequences of not doing so. *I've got to eat now!*

But where?

Well, there was Lespinasse, with its extravagant floral displays. Or she might dine at La Grenouille, which was no less conveniently located, and would erode the increasingly depleted financial resources of one Arthur Vandameer no less severely. There was Alain Ducasse and La Côte Basque, and as Allison contemplated the enormity of the bill she could with a bite of *fois gras* and a sip of Chateau Haut-Brion bloat out of all human proportion, she found herself fondling her Platinum American Express card with tingling delight, despite the fact that it had nearly lost its characteristic sheen as specialist after specialist had, with wild abandon, swiped its slender plastic torso through the welcoming slit of the credit card machine.

Hm, Allison thought. She cast her eyes toward the Plaza. No way would she be allowed into the ebony darkness of its fabled Oak Room. Besides, in her present condition of near famishment, along with hunger's accompanying affliction, beer nuts would be about as helpful as a black bean burrito.

Where then? Allison mused as her eyes swept the crowded Plaza, moving from the grand hotel's towering façade, across the limousine-lined driveway, over to the circular fountain, and finally to Fifth Avenue where, to her astonishment, the very male whom she could— though not without syntactical complexity—no longer assume to be tightly wrapped around her little finger was, at that moment being rudely tugged forward by the very peanut whose Roy he evidently was.

Now where could they be going, Allison wondered as Roy and Mr. Salty abruptly turned and headed south down Fifth Avenue.

A terrible possibility dawned in Allison's now furiously working mind.

What if Roy Bumble had been right? What if Mr. Salty worked for Arthur Vandameer? Worse still, what if that very peanut was leading the aforementioned Roy to the studios of WNIN, where, she darkly surmised, Roy would confess to everything, name herself as instigator of the plot, and thus forever dash any hope of the Best Director Award.

No! Allison cried inwardly, and on that word, took off in guarded, but steely-eyed, pursuit.

THALES' WATER TORTURE

Harry Stumbo

Harry gazed wistfully at the mercifully dingy porno shop across from Port Authority, one of the very few that still graced what had once been New York's seediest neighborhood.

"What do you think, couple inches across, right?" Cheekie asked as he once again massaged the enormous bump that rose horn-like from the center of his brow.

Harry noted that Cheekie's eyes were still quite disconcertingly crossed, but saw no reason to so inform the aforementioned, and clearly undisconcerted, Cheekie.

And so Harry returned to the subject about which he had been mentally engaged for the last few minutes. "Change," he said.

Cheekie glanced toward the corner window of Duane Reed before which apothecary window he casually lounged, and in which he now caught his battered reflection in the glass, then, spurred to calculation, glanced at his watch. "It could be a record," he crowed happily. "Eyes still crossed after forty-eight minutes." He laughed. "That frigging peanut really tagged me."

Harry held his gaze on the pornography shop. He had no interest in pornography, but briefly considered buying several disgusting tapes in hopes of aiding VIDEO XXX in its doubtlessly uphill battle to pay the cruelly augmented rent that had previously sealed the fate of nearly all such similarly sleazy and disreputable enterprises in the area, the nastiest of which (dubbed "Humper Heaven" by its discreetly rain-coated aficionados) had, as Harry gloomily recalled now, already been replaced by—dear God—a Starbucks!

"You were saying?" Cheekie asked.

Harry chose not to return to the original subject of his prior reflection, and instead focused on the latest of his now presumably unsuccessful business entanglements. "Moon," he said.

"Yeah," Cheekie admitted, his admiring gaze once more drawn to the impressive black-eyed shiner that he clearly thought accessorized quite well not only with the ill-turned eyes, but the bump that seemed still to be expanding across his otherwise regrettably unmarked brow. "We still got a job to do."

"Ideas?" Harry inquired.

"Ask Moon," Cheekie replied.

"Where?"

"Cell phone."

Harry did as Cheekie suggested, drew the phone from his shirt pocket and dialed Charlie Moon.

"Harry," Harry said, paused a moment, then added. "Okay."

Cheekie nodded.

"Where?" Harry asked into the phone.

Cheekie cocked his ear attentively.

"Now?" Harry asked, again into the phone.

Cheekie nodded confidently.

"Ten minutes," Harry said, then closed the phone.

Cheekie smiled. "Now we're getting somewhere," he said.

Charlie Moon

Even though he'd just ordered Harry Stumbo and Cheekie Putoyna to close ranks and proceed toward the offices and studios of WNIN, Charlie still wasn't exactly sure in which capacity he wished to use them.

In fact, at the present moment, only one thing was clear in Charlie's mind.

He had to do something!

Why?

Because during the last several minutes of brutally distended Q&A with Goonie Castillo de la Mancha Diaz, a slender series of facts had determinedly been rescued from the otherwise impenetrable fog. Facts which, in the aggregate, were so disturbing that when collected together to form a single unavoidable conclusion, they had sent a continually reverberating shiver down the otherwise steely spine of one Charles W. Moon.

Fact 1)   Goonie Castillo de La Mancha Diaz had been invited to appear on Arthur Vandameer's show.

Fact 2)   Arthur Vandameer was going to interview the aforementioned Goonie for a full hour.

Fact 3) The subject of that interview was going to be the impending nuptials of Goonie Castillo de la Mancha Diaz and Allison Vandameer.

These three woefully incontestable facts had immediately led to the three suppositions that even now whipped about in Charlie's mind, suppositions that, if proven true, contained all the destructive possibility of briefcase-nukes.

Supposition 1)   The Goonie interview might not end with Goonie's beheading.

Supposition 2)   The Goonie interview might end with Arthur Vandameer's gracious and heartfelt acceptance of the aforementioned Goonie as his son-in-law.

Supposition 3)   The aforementioned acceptance might well signal an unexpected and wholly alarming sea-change in Arthur Vandameer, a personal commitment to weepy, hand-wringing, knee-jerk left-wing values sufficient to transform every feature of Arthur's public and private life.

In other words, Arthur Vandameer might actually begin to live according to the weepy, hand-wringing, knee-jerk, left-wing values he had for thirty years espoused.

*   *   *

And what was so horrible about such gracious and heartfelt conversion?

The possibilities were as boundless as they were appalling:

1) Despising educational elitism, Arthur might send Allison to a public school.
2) Despising the injustice of inherited wealth, Arthur might turn over his assets to one of many malevolent charities.
3) Despising the filthy lucre of the capitalist system, Arthur might join the ranks of migrant labor.
4) Despising the tax advantages of the rich, Arthur might—oh my God!—file the Short Form.

Charlie's mind reeled with the horrible vision of Arthur Vandameer, the designated Loudmouth of American Liberalism, suddenly divested of the one characteristic upon which he, Charlie, had always relied in his long battle with pinko-lefty-progressives.

For it could not be doubted, as Charlie didn't doubt, that if Arthur Vandameer suddenly led the liberal vanguard in this direction, it would surely put a bullet in the head of the one tried and true fact of life that had served as the unwavering basis of Charlie's political conviction, the one thing upon which he had always counted in his withering assault on Arthur Vandermeer and his left-leaning comrades. It would remove from play the gleaming spear upon which he had time and again impaled the aforementioned comrades.

The spear, that is, of LIBERAL HYPOCRISY!

For what attack could Charlie possibly mount against Arthur Vandameer if all of a sudden Arthur actually embraced a life devoid of contradiction? Tagging liberal hypocrisy had always been easy. Like shooting whales in a barrel. Every liberal had that single huge, red-eyed target emblazoned upon his forehead. As a matter of fact, Charlie shuddered to recall, for the last forty years he had hardly been able to speak the noun "hypocrisy" without attaching the necessary and wholly justifiable adjective "liberal."

BUT NOW ALL OF THAT MIGHT BE TAKEN AWAY!

"No!" Charlie whispered vehemently just as the very specter of Arthur Vandameer's unwelcome personal reformation swept past the Green Room, his hawkish mien barely more than a jagged silhouette, but sufficient for Charlie to realize that Arthur Vandameer was at this electric instant making his way down the corridor, toward the now hastily revamped set of the newly titled *Left of Mental*.

Arthur Vandameer

Arthur stared at the hastily revamped set of the newly titled *Left of Mental*. He could not decide which of its elements appalled him more. There was the large photograph of Arthur, but with a large egg now plastered on his forehead, the yellow yolk of which dripped in gooey pulsing yellow neon down the bridge of his nose, where it dropped yet again to form an equally gooey yellow pool upon his chin.

"Egg on your face, get it, son?" Roland Fitzwater crowed loudly as he stepped up behind Arthur. This comment was followed by a hearty slap on the back, which was, itself, followed by the familiar booming voice. "*Left of Mental* is going to be the liveliest, no holds barred political show this country has ever seen, my boy." His eyes swept toward another design which showed Arthur pressing an enormous cream pie into the hugely grinning features of Jerry Falwell. "It's going to be *Crossfire* meets *Saturday Night Live*." He considered this, then added, "No, even better. It's *Nightline* meets *Jackass*." He shrugged. "Anyway, you get the message, Artie."

The head of Arthur Vandameer rotated leftward like a melon on a broomstick. "Artie?" the head inquired.

"Yeah, we thought we'd put a more casual spin on things . . . Artie," Roland said. "So it's going to be *Left of Mental . . . with Artie V.*" He grinned expansively. "Great, right?"

The mouth of the newly christened Artie V. dropped widely agape. "But . . . but. . . ."

"Goonie's in the Green Room," Roland cried. "Oh, and by the way, we've added a studio audience."

"Audience?" Arthur gasped. "But I've never had a . . ." He glanced to the left, where a small army of stagehands was now hastily arranging row after row of metal chairs. "You mean . . . tonight?"

"What better time, Artie?" Roland responded with a loud laugh.

"And we're going . . . live?"

"Well, of course," Fitzwater yelped. "Hell, son,

what's the point of live ambush television if nobody gets caught with his pants around his ankles?" His laughter pealed over the now assembled metal chairs. "I mean, you don't tip over the outhouse if nobody's in it."

"But it's not supposed to be the host who's in . . ."

"That's the glory of this new idea, Artie," Fitzwater grandly interrupted. "That even the host can hit the fan."

"Fan?"

"I'm telling you, Artie," Roland beamed. "The audience will really yuk it up!"

"Yuk it up?" Arthur whined. "But that's not . . ."

"Decline," Roland gravely intoned, his eyes now narrowing into twin threatening slits.

"But . . ."

"Goonie's in the Green Room," Roland repeated significantly. He glanced at his watch. "Thirty minutes to air," he added, and with those words vanished into a blue smoke, vanished with such magical rapidity in fact that Arthur had no time to blurt the pregnant words "Purple Slinky," thus leaving the aforementioned Arthur "Artie V" Vandameer standing, more or less in shock, before the brightly colored set of *Left of Mental*.

HEIDEGGER'S THROWNESS

Roy Stumbo

"That's the way to get in," Bea Bumble announced as she came to a halt at the corner of 46th and Sixth Avenue. She flourished the cane toward a large hand-scrawled sandwich board currently borne by what seemed to Roy a clearly deranged homeless person.

Roy glanced at the sandwich board, and with sinking heart, read its generous offer to seat "any and all" as audience members for *Left of Mental with Artie V.*

"How do you get into the audience?" Bea asked as she stepped up to the sandwich board.

The sandwich board appeared not in the least to notice that it had just been so addressed by a peanut.

"Foist elevator ta da lef," the sandwich board instructed, one hand raised, a single finger indicating the impressively marbled entrance of WNIN.

Thus instructed, Bea Bumble whirled leftward, Roy trudging at her side while his mind grimly contemplated the consequences of his imminent coming clean, all of which involved decidedly unpleasant nocturnal romps with the distantly aforementioned Bull Diablo.

"Do I have to?" Roy pleaded as Bea Bumble sped

forward with ever-increasing velocity toward yet another hastily scrawled sign, this one in the still impressively marbled lobby of WNIN, and which pointedly directed prospective audience members of *Left of Mental* to elevator number five.

"Yes, you do, Roy," Bea Bumble answered, her eyes glittering from the dark and cavernous depths of Mr. Salty. "You got to say you're sorry!"

"But . . . but . . ."

"You got to say you're sorry!" Bea repeated fiercely, her words all but drowned out by some sort of commotion, voices echoing loudly from marble wall to marble wall, so that as the doors of elevator five closed, Roy was only able to make out the single shouted interrogative, "You deaf or just stupid?"

Harry Stumbo

"You deaf or just stupid!" Cheekie screamed into the face of WNIN's imposing Chief of Security.

"Please don't raise your voice, sir," the Chief of Security responded with an unexpected politeness that Cheekie clearly considered unconscionably provocative.

"Oh yeah?" Cheekie demanded, despite the firm, restraining hand Harry had placed on his, Cheekie's, shoulder. "You the limp-dicked pansy that's gonna stop me, you numbnuts-bug-humper."

"Jeez," Harry groaned, now fully expecting the aforementioned bug-humper to follow-up his latest restrained and quite polite remark with a sudden lurch, followed by a seizure, followed by a kick, which moves when collectively administered would no doubt transport Cheekie through the nearest plate glass window.

"You're going to have to leave, sir," the Chief of Security said, his face now sufficiently crimson to entice a charging bull.

"I ain't going no-frigging-where," Cheekie shouted.

"Oh yes you are."

Cheekie seemed confused by the fact that these last four words had been spoken without the Chief of Security in the slightest moving his lips.

"You're going to be in the audience of our new show, *Left of Mental*."

Same voice. Same lack of moving lips.

Cheekie put two and two together, turned away from the Chief and settled his eyes on a guy in a large white cowboy hat.

"Roland Fitzwater," the Cowboy Hat said. He stretched out his hand. "You, my dear fellow, have exactly the kind of, shall we say, volatility I'm looking for in tonight's audience."

Cheekie looked at Harry.

Harry nodded.

"What are you talking about?" Cheekie challenged.

"My good man, you're wasting a truly superior offensiveness on objects far less deserving of such powers than a poor, underpaid security officer. What you need, dear boy, is SOMEBODY BIG!"

Cheekie's eyes glittered with the irresistible possibility of long-term hospitalization. "Yeah?" he sputtered.

"Absolutely," the Cowboy Hat said. "Why, son, in

this very building, your capacity for giving monstrous and unreasoning insult can be used to the maximum."

Cheekie blinked rapidly. "Oh yeah?" he aforementionedly, and with cruel indifference to the rules of adverbial usage, sputtered.

"My point, son," the Cowboy Hat said, "is that there is a person in this building far bigger than my poor Chief of Security, a person far more worthy of your incontestable ability to heckle and offend."

"Bigger?" Cheekie mused with delicious anticipation. "How big is this frigging guy?"

"Huge," the Cowboy Hat said assuredly. "And I'd be more than pleased to arrange the meeting." With a flourish, he drew Cheekie beneath his arm. "Allow me to escort you to the elevator." He glanced back at the gathering crowd of people who wished to attend the newly conceived *Left of Mental*. "And let those two in the audience, as well," he called to the security guard, nodding toward a man in an ornate doorman's uniform and a rather imposing peanut, "They'll be perfect."

Allison Vandameer

Allison Vandameer watched aghast as Roy Bumble and Mr. Salty were pulled from the ranks of audience hopefuls and hustled toward the waiting doors of elevator five.

"I'm Allison Vandameer," Allison Vandermeer said as she stepped up to a large and still red-faced security officer who looked oddly shaken, though no less determined to block her way. "Arthur Vandameer's daughter."

"I see," the security guard said. "Do you have identification?"

Allison did, in fact, have identification, and the fierce approach of yet another gas attack propelled her to reach for it with lightning speed. "Here it is," she said, with both teeth and sphincters clinched.

The security guard mulled over Allison's beautifully engraved invitation to Buffy Sedgewick-Mellon's debutante ball.

"This is not an ID," he observed with a look that struck Allison as perilously near disdainful.

In response, she unclenched her teeth, but maintained strict control over the aforementioned sphincters. "My father is Arthur Vandameer," she proclaimed once again. "He has a show here. *Speaking Truth to Power.*"

The security guard appeared to have no discernible interest in either Arthur Vandameer or his show.

"Do you have any other kind of identification?" he dutifully inquired.

Allison felt a hideous balloon of gas cruelly press its case toward the only known route of egress. "Jeez," she cried, "Let me in!"

The security guard did no such thing. "I'm sorry, Miss."

Allison tensed her body against the impending doom, and somehow managed to delay it while she frantically fished about in the elegant Prada handbag she'd purchased, more or less on a whim, only a few short hours before.

"Here," she said, thrusting her Trinity School student ID toward the security guard, as well as her Amex-Platinum, and finally, with cutting embarrassment, her regrettably unimpressive MasterCard, a card neither gold nor platinum, and CERTAINLY NOT the elegantly black Centurion that nestled auspiciously in Arthur's Armani wallet, but in fact a card, the aforementioned neither gold nor platinum Mastercharge, so lacking in prestige that she'd actually seen it proffered by people who had without doubt entered the country illegally.

The security guard slowly perused the items thus offered and by some calculus known only to himself decided that they did, at least collectively, meet the ID requirements for admission to *Left of Mental*. "Elevator Five," he said.

Mercifully, as Allison noted as she sped away, Elevator Five was empty, a circumstance she greeted with the pressing expectation of impending, and with any luck wholly silent, relief.

HEGEL, MARX AND THE BIPOLAR PROBLEM

Charlie Moon

Charlie Moon was confused.

And why shouldn't he be?

For here he stood, facing the now completely reconstituted set of *Left of Mental*, watching from the shadows as Arthur Vandameer dejectedly took his seat at a desk which now looked less like a desk than a barker's stand on Coney Island, complete with pulsing red, white and blue lights.

What is this? Charlie wondered, his consternation only intensifying as the studio audience was led into the room, and there among them, were none other than Harry Stumbo, Cheekie Putonya, Allison Vandameer, and the Sherry-Netherland guy, the latter sternly directed to his seat by, of all things, an indisputably imposing peanut.

What is this? Charlie wondered yet again, his gaze now returning to the aforementioned but no less than previously dejected Arthur Vandameer.

Charlie's mind raced to develop a theory that might explain such a confounding convergence of humanity that did not involve organ harvesting by alien lifeforms.

What Vast Right-Wing Conspiracy could explain such a gathering? How could it be that the aforementioned human confluence could have—Charlie couldn't think of a verb sufficient to convey the meaning he sought, and thus made one up on the spot—confluded?

Time, Charlie thought, time was what he needed to straighten out the baffling vision which confronted him from the eighteen rows of metal chairs in which the audience now sat in stillness, save for the violently squirming figure of Allison Vandameer, whose plainly pinched and troubled features made her look as if she were contemplating nothing less cataclysmic than the end of time.

But that very, and until now never aforementioned time, ever in short supply, was even more shortly supplied at that moment, a truth made distressingly evident, as Charlie observed, by the decidedly shambling approach of Goonie Castillo de la Mancha Diaz, who was at that precise instant being led like a condemned felon from the Green Room to the backstage position from which, Charlie assumed, he would make his entrance onto the carnival boardwalk set of *Left of Mental*.

Charlie tried to think, but suddenly a burst of canned music swept through the studio, startling the audience, the blare of a calliope so loud it rattled the camera lenses, a cacophony immediately followed by the similarly recorded introduction of "Joselito Castillo de la Mancha Diaz" as the first guest of *Left of Mental*, hosted by *Artie V.*

Goonie's small brown eyes slid over to Charlie.

"No way I'm eating no bull balls," he whispered vehemently.

Then, no less suddenly than the blare of the calliope, a withering shaft of light swept over the aforementioned Goonie as a formerly unseen hand abruptly pushed him forward so that he all but staggered onto the fiendishly glittering set where he momentarily froze, then inched forward, blearily glancing about until he finally reached the empty seat that faced none other than the newly christened Artie V.

"Uh, welcome . . . Joselito," Arthur stammered, his own eyes now casting about, as if trying to convince himself that it was all a nightmare from which he might suddenly awaken. "How are . . . you today?"

Goonie's face seemed to pale at the indecipherable depth of Artie V.'s introductory interrogative, an indication, it seemed to Charlie, that as to the present condition of himself, the aforementioned Goonie remained characteristically clueless.

"Okay . . . well," Arthur said, clearly at a loss as his eyes fell desperately upon the blank sheet before him. For what questions could he have possibly prepared for the Goonie Castillo de la Mancha Diaz that did not involve a skateboard. "You're . . . Joselito."

"Well . . . duh!" Goonie said softly.

"What?" Arthur inquired.

"Even I know that," Goonie replied.

The audience laughed, and Charlie noticed that a few of them appeared suddenly to relax, except, as he equally noticed, the still violently squirming figure of Allison Vandameer.

"Yes," Arthur said, "Of course." His eyes appeared to cross briefly, then resume their forward gaze. "Of course," he repeated.

Of course what? Charlie wondered, waiting impatiently now for Arthur to seize the moment, take back the reins of his show . . . DO SOMETHING!

"Uh, right," Arthur muttered.

JEEZ, Charlie thought, JEEZ!

"Okay," Arthur sputtered. "Okay, let's talk about . . . you . . . uh . . . Joselito. . . ."

"That you know as Goonie," Goonie said, in response to which the audience chuckled.

"Goonie, yes," Arthur said, clearly heedless of the aforementioned collective chuckle, and thus still bent upon interviewing Joselito Castillo de la Mancha Diaz that he knew as Goonie as if Goonie were, say, Henry Kissinger. "Anyway, uh . . . tell me . . . what is your . . . favorite subject . . . in . . . school . . . uh . . . Goonie?"

Goonie looked utterly relieved by the question. He grinned proudly. "Lunch," he declared. "Especially fish sticks."

The audience laughed again . . . except of course for the continually squirming Allison.

"Yes, right," Arthur stammered. "Lunch."

Charlie moaned. Dear God, if this went on for ten more seconds, he thought, Roland Fitzwater would pull the plug, and Arthur Vandameer would disappear from television faster than a selfless thought from Bill Clinton's mind. But that couldn't happen, he reminded himself, because it was all a plot, this whole charade, a plot hatched by Fitzwater and Vandameer, a plot hatched to destroy one Charles W. Moon, and thus a plot he, the aforementioned Charles W., HAD TO FIGURE OUT FAST!

"I mean . . ." Arthur went on haltingly. "Besides . . . lunch."

Goonie looked as if he'd just been asked to calculate the orbital speed of Pluto. "Besides . . . lunch?"

Charlie slapped his brow loudly with an open hand, but the audience only laughed, now more loudly than before, as a general levity suddenly gave rise to a dreadful possibility in Charlie's perfervid brain.

IF *LEFT OF MENTAL* GOT GOOD RATINGS, COULD *RIGHT OF MENTAL* BE FAR BEHIND?

Charlie instantly envisioned George Will spinning a large wheel festooned with portraits of eminent conservative thinkers. Dear God, he thought, as the audience burst out laughing at some remark Charlie's own frantic mental processes had briefly blocked from entry.

Charlie's gaze swept toward the audience, whose members—save for Allison Vandameer, of course— were presently bent over in laughter while Arthur Vandameer stared about vacantly. Never had the Loudmouth of Liberalism looked more entirely closed-mouth. Sitting at the garishly lighted desk, peering at the enormous portrait of his egg-splattered face, the esteemed Arthur Vandameer appeared for the first time in his loud-mouthed life to be positively silenced.

SILENCED?

Arthur Vandameer . . . SILENCED?

Charlie gasped as the truth dawned, and the real plot, far more insidious than any Charlie had previously imagined, was in a flash revealed. The algebra was as simple as it was devastating. If Arthur Vandameer were silenced, then Charles W. Moon would be no less immediately rendered mute.

Why?

The answer was obvious.

Without idiotic liberals, the nation would have no further need for idiotic conservatives!

NO ARTHUR MEANT NO CHARLIE!

It was as simple as that.

And if that happened, who would then take over a great nation's political discourse?

Again the answer was simple.

MODERATES!

So that was it, Charlie thought, both he and Arthur Vandameer were about to be undone by a Vast Moderate Conspiracy!

Suddenly Charlie envisioned himself and Arthur Vandameer being chased through the woods by a torch-lit mob of perfectly reasonable people.

And what would this mob demand of the aforementioned Charlie and Arthur once they'd run them down and strapped them to the stake? What, in their burning obsession to change the political discussion of a great nation, would they insist upon with a fanatical determination?

Something unbearable: BALANCED OPINION!

It was a nightmarish vision, and Charlie all but screamed at the horrible notion that the country he loved might be rudely denied the snarling rancor of both left and right-wing media mutts. Where would all

those rhetorical half-truths go, those loaded questions
and slanted statistics, the phony moral posturing and
false accusations, the whole boiling cauldron of intem-
perate rhetoric and school-yard bickering, where
would all that go if moderation took the day, bringing
with it, as Charlie knew it would, a wholly impermissi-
ble civility, politeness, statesmanship, personal grace,
all of which, when taken together, would doubtlessly
bestow upon political debate an entirely unacceptable
sense of gravity.

Which hideous spectacle now gave rise to the question of the moment as it was posed in Charlie's wildly
teeming mind. Namely, how could this radical
onslaught of political solemnity be stopped?

Only one way, Charlie decided. By making sure that
Arthur Vandameer's ass DID NOT GO DOWN IN
FLAMES!

And so, Charlie thought for the third time in a few
short hours, to horse!

Arthur Vandameer

Arthur could not believe his eyes.

The recorded announcement had just proclaimed
Left of Mental's first commercial break when out of the
backstage shadows stepped no less than Charles W.
Moon, apparently fired with purpose, and whose bold
stride transported him immediately to Goonie's side.

"Goonie," Charlie said loudly. "It's not bull balls."

Goonie's features locked in dread, as Charlie leaned
forward and whispered.

"It's *mierda*," Charlie said, using one of the three words he knew in Spanish.

"*Mierda?*" Goonie yelped.

". . . *de vaca*," Charlie added, using the final two words he knew in Spanish.

"NOOOOOO!" Goonie cried, his body lifting like a rocket from his chair, then whirling first right, then left, until he chose a direction (left), and rushed away, arms flapping like unfledged wings as he raced, still screaming, down the adjoining corridor.

"Fifteen seconds," a disembodied voice cried.

Arthur stared at Charlie wordlessly as he, Charlie, slid into the seat most recently occupied by Goonie Castillo de la Mancha Diaz.

"Ten seconds."

Charlie leaned forward and stared Arthur directly in the eye.

"Five seconds."

Arthur leaned forward and stared Charlie directly in the eye.

"Four."

"Three."

"Two."

"One."

"Uh," Arthur began. "I have a surprise . . . guest."

Charlie smiled as the small red light went on and he glimpsed himself on camera. He liked what he saw, a face emboldened by the grand purpose of rescuing the Republic from the evil grasp of rhetorical restraint.

"My guest is Charles W. Moon," Arthur intoned, now winglessly winging it. "And I have to say that Mr.

Moon and I have agreed on almost nothing in our respective careers, and that . . ."

"True enough, Arthur," Charlie interrupted loudly, cocking his head to the right. "But I'm confident in saying that we can surely agree on one thing." He paused and looked dead-eye into the camera. "Moderation must be stamped out!"

Arthur's lips parted silently.

"Those voices that shout down our shouting," Charlie added. "Call on us to be temperate in our remarks. Moderates of every stripe."

"Moderates?" Arthur repeated gingerly. "You mean . . ."

"I mean the very people, my dear friend," Charlie steamed on. "The very people who wish to extinguish a great beacon of left-wing balderdash like yourself."

"Uh . . ." Arthur stammered . . . "Me?"

"You, indeed, sir," Charlie continued, "For who else can claim to be so thoroughly bloated with cockamamie ideas? Who else has steadfastly maintained one place on television where a man can find all he can possible stomach by way of unadulterated left-wing horse hockey?" He drew in a long breath. "I salute you, sir."

Arthur's eyes popped. "You . . . what?"

"I salute the many years of sacrifice that you, Arthur Vandameer, have given to spreading pure nonsense from sea to shining sea." He faced the audience. "AM I RIGHT?"

The audience burst into applause.

"Let us not forget," Charlie cried. "That this man,

alone among sentient beings, ACTUALLY BELIEVES THAT O.J. DIDN'T DO IT!"

Arthur swallowed hard. "I'm not sure I agree that. . . ."

"Imagine, ladies and gentleman," Charlie continued, now using hand signals to rev the audience toward yet greater remonstrance. "Imagine the effort it takes to spew forth opinions so utterly without reference to earthbound experience, so wholly in contradiction to human nature, opinions, in short, that would cross the eyes of lesser mortals. These farfetched and feckless notions, dear viewers, have been the stock-in-trade of our brave host." Charlie began to clap his hands loudly. "And I believe that deserves a loud and enthusiastic round of applause."

The audience responded with a loud and enthusiastic round of applause, punctuated with cheers of "Hurrah" and "Bravo," the first two rows now leaping from their metal chairs, along with, as Charlie noticed, the doorman of the Sherry-Netherland, who in a moment of what appeared to be religious conversation, shouted a boisterous and heartfelt, "I'M SORRY!"

"So, I'm here to say that it takes a Big, Big Man to come into eight million homes each night and make a complete ASS of himself!" Charlie cried. "A BIG BIG MAN."

"Yeah?" a hostile voice called from the audience. "How big?"

Arthur turned to see a small man with oddly crossed eyes standing on his chair, his lower arm held tightly within the grasp of a second man.

"You know him?" Arthur asked frantically as

Cheekie broke free of Harry Stumbo's grasp and stormed toward the stage.

"Uh," Charlie gasped, his eyes riveted upon the scene before him, the whole audience instantly on its feet, save for Allison Vandameer, who now appeared to be squirming even more desperately, her eyes all but popped as if she were being hideously inflated by a mercilessly determined air hose.

"So how big are you?" Cheekie yelled as he drew in upon Arthur's desk, his fists clenched, a murderous glare in his still crossed eyes.

Arthur's eyes widened in horror. "What?"

Cheekie continued to storm forward. "You deaf or just stupid?" he cried, now gathering speed as he bulled forward, a little train that quite obviously could.

"Cheekie, don't!" Charlie cried.

But too late, as Cheekie, now fully on camera, but no less bent upon confronting Arthur Vandameer, lunged violently toward the aforementioned Arthur, his crossed eyes like cross-hairs, he, Cheekie, the avenging weapon, Arthur now certain to receive the blast of that all too human weaponry when . . . all of a sudden. . . .

BRRRRRRRRRRRRRRT!

All action froze, save for the flashing movement of Charlie's eyes toward the locus of the aforementioned, an undeniably familiar explosion of sound, at which locus he spied Allison Vandameer, her face glowing bright red, as if suddenly spotted by a cruelly crimson light.

EPILOGUE

FORTY
MINUTES
LATER

EPILOGUES DON'T HAVE CHAPTER TITLES

Roy Bumble

Roy sat in the rumbling subway car, bound for Queens, his wife Bea in peanut form beside him.

"I wanted to say more," Roy told her, lying though his teeth. "I wanted to tell Mr. Vandameer the whole story."

Mr. Salty's white glove closed around Roy's stubby fingers. "You did enough, sweetheart," Bea Bumble said. "Besides, after the . . . that . . . well . . . people were in a hurry to get out."

That much was true, Roy recalled. In fact, he was reasonably sure that nothing less than a surging wall of flame could have driven the audience from the set of *Left of Mental* any faster than the wholly unexpected explosion of sound which had terminated the aforementioned program well before its scheduled end.

"Anyway," Roy said. "I wanted to come clean."

"I'm sure you did," Bea Bumble said.

Roy leaned back, closed his eyes, and felt the warm embrace of a slender peanut arm as it gathered him to its peanut bosom. This, he decided, was happiness, just to be humble Roy Bumble, a guy from Queens.

Harry Stumbo

"Dewar's," Harry said.

"Two," Cheekie added.

Felix the Barkeep poured.

"Loud," Harry said.

"Whoa!" Cheekie added.

"Who?"

Cheekie shrugged.

"Eyes," Harry said.

"Uncrossed?"

Harry nodded.

Cheekie glanced at his watch. "Record," he said triumphantly, then peered about until his grateful gaze fell upon an enormous construction worker who sat at the far end of the bar. "For now."

Harry watched as Cheekie slid off the stool and made his way toward the construction worker. He smiled, pleased that even in a lamentably changing world, some things never changed.

Arthur Vandameer

Arthur sat near the Sherman statue, Allison at his side.

"You saved me," he said.

Allison nodded.

"That guy was going to kill me."

Allison nodded.

"You okay?" Arthur asked.

Allison glanced toward the statue. "Nero made it a law," she said. "You had to . . . do it. It wasn't healthy not to, so Nero made it a law that you had to. Even at the table."

Arthur stared at Allison wonderingly. "Where did you learn that?" he marveled.

"In Suetonious, I think," Allison replied.

Arthur's lips parted in both astonishment and admiration. "When did you read Suetonious?"

"Just after I finished Gibbon's *Decline and Fall*," Allison answered matter-of-factly.

"Why didn't you tell me that you . . ." He stopped, placed his arm around his daughter's shoulder and drew her to his side. "So, you want to make movies," he said.

Charlie Moon

Charlie sat down at his desk at the *Register* and considered what he might do next. One thing was sure, there'd be no pube-scoop. Try as he might, there was no way this story could get past the ever vigilant taste-mongers within the editorial department. He could just hear Maury Rittenour's squeaky little voice, the note of offense that would certainly be couched within the squeak, *You can't write about THAT!*

He shook his head disconsolately as he faced the fact. There were just certain things you couldn't write about. And to write about something other than THAT would be to falsify the story.

Hm, Charlie thought, falsify the story? Instead of what actually happened, maybe have the set collapse, a light explode, the result being the same; namely that all hell broke loose, Cheekie toppling over Arthur Vandameer's desk, the audience scrambling for cover, everyone running from what they knew had done it, that huge peanut!

Not bad, Charlie thought as he considered this new ending. Of course it wasn't exactly true. As a matter of fact it wasn't true at all. He considered certain journalists who had recently been exposed for creating composite characters or making things up entirely. A couple of them were now regulars on TV talking their talking heads off on the issues of the day. He smiled. *Yeah*, he thought, *with just the right amount of "moral flexibility," a guy could be a star.*

Madelyn Boyd

Madelyn sat silently before her flat-screen television and watched the press coverage of what the media feeding frenzy was now calling the "WNIN Implosion."

On screen, Roland Fitzwater, surrounded by reporters and madly whirling about like a big fat tuna in a pool of starving sharks, was frantically trying to explain what had happened on the set of *Left of Mental.*

"It was all a joke, boys," he declared. "A little April Fools' joke on . . . you guys!"

From the mob of microphone-armed reporters, a lone voice pointed out the salient and by no means irrelevant fact that July 1 was not April Fools' Day.

"But that's what makes it so funny," Roland countered with a wide, wholly disingenuous cackle. "Get it? To have an April Fools' joke when it's not April Fools' Day. That's a real April Fools' Day joke."

The crowd of reporters stared at Roland blankly,

trying to untwist the coiled tail of his entirely specious reasoning.

Next came Arthur Vandameer, his hair looking as if it had been blown dry in an wind-tunnel, furiously trying to explain that none of it was his fault to the same famished gaggle of reporters who'd previously cut Roland off at the pass. "I never wanted to change the format of the show," Arthur whined. "All of this was a complete surprise to me . . . especially the . . . guests!"

"You didn't know who was going to be on your show?" one of the reporters shouted.

Arthur shook his head violently. "Nothing," he bawled. "I knew nothing!"

And finally to Charlie Moon, equally surrounded, and no less in squirming mode, as he attempted to explain his otherwise inexplicable appearance on *Left of Mental.* "I fainted," he said. "And the next thing I knew. . . ."

Madelyn heaved a world-weary sigh at the comic yet curiously earnest spectacle before her. Everyone was on his own, on the loose, chasing his own dream. And so, nothing would ever be finished in this most American of towns, or lost, or exhausted, or defeated...ever. Suddenly she felt an odd and wholly uncharacteristic wave of affection sweep over her. *What else would you expect,* she asked herself, as she turned off the aforementioned flat-screen television, and thus rendered still and silent the madcap antics of her kind, *New Yorkers.*